STORIES TOTO TOLD ME

Fr. Rolfe (Baron Corvo)

STORIES TOTO TOLD ME

by

FREDERICK ROLFE
(BARON CORVO)

Edited with an introduction and notes by
EDMUND MILLER

VALANCOURT BOOKS

Stories Toto Told Me by Baron Corvo
First published in 1898 by John Lane
First Valancourt Books edition 2008

Library of Congress Cataloging-in-Publication Data

Rolfe, Frederick, 1860-1913.
 Stories Toto told me / by Frederick Rolfe (Baron Corvo) ;
edited with an introduction and notes by Edmund Miller. – 1st
Valancourt Books ed.
      p. cm.
 Includes bibliographical references (p.   ).
 ISBN 1-934555-58-4 (alk. paper)
 I. Title.
 PR5236.R27S76 2008
 823'.8–DC22

                                    2008030324

Published by Valancourt Books
http://www.valancourtbooks.com

CONTENTS

INTRODUCTION

FREDERICK WILLIAM ROLFE, who sometimes expanded his name to Frederick William Serafino Austin Lewis Mary Rolfe and often wrote as Baron Corvo, was born on 22 July 1860 in London. Although he had obviously developed a strong interest in learning in his youth, he left school early in his teens. Having converted to Roman Catholicism, he eked out a living as an artist, a photographer, even a school teacher.

In 1880 he published the poetry chapbook *Tarcissus* and began writing to add to his income. Six stories by Corvo narrated primarily in the voice of an Italian servant boy were published in the literary magazine *The Yellow Book*. The magazine became a flashpoint of fin de siècle decadence, and publication in this organ brought with it a good deal of visibility, leading in 1898 to publication of the stories as the book *Stories Toto Told Me* reprinted here. These stories were revised and twenty-four were added to make *In His Own Image*, which appeared in 1901. In *Stories Toto Told Me*, the primary narrator of the stories, simultaneously naïve and precocious, is an idealized companion for the bachelor Englishman who employs him. The boy is charming and loquacious with an anecdote for all occasions.

But writing never provided a regular income, and Rolfe's (or Corvo's) real desire was ordination. When his vocation was questioned—apparently because of his perceived homosexual sensibility—he took a twenty-year vow of chastity. His obsession with

Roman Catholicism is clear in a group of works begun at this time. These works show the distinctive characteristics of a Corvine prose style with self-consciously arcane vocabulary and a focus on Renaissance historical subjects. The works also show an insistence on the good works of the notorious Borgia family. The 1901 book *Chronicles of the House of Borgia* presents sympathetic portraits of Pope Alexander VI, of Lucretia, and of Cesare (whose Borgia paternity Corvo perversely doubts). There is evidence of extensive historical research in this work although the rehabilitation of the Borgias has not won many converts. A related novel is the 1905 *Don Tarquinio: A Kataleptic Phantasmatic Romance*, a careful reconstruction of one day in the life of a condottiere (or soldier of fortune). A similar novel written in prose even more baroque is *Don Renato: An Ideal Content* (printed in 1909 but not released for sale until 1963).

Corvo also tried collaboration during this period. *Hubert's Arthur* with C. H. C. Pirie-Gordon was completed although not published until 1935. It is an imagined life of Arthur, Duke of Brittany, had he escaped death at the hands of King John. Arthur becomes a crusader, marries the heiress of the Kingdom of Jerusalem, and returns to fight for the English crown in trial by combat with John's son, his historical successor King Henry III. Another collaboration with Pirie-Gordon is *The Weird of the Wanderer* (1912), a tale of reincarnation.

At the end of the term of self-abnegation represented by the vow of chastity, Corvo proved to his own satisfaction his worthiness of ordination, but his failure to be ordained in fact had two consequences. One was personal. He accepted his sexual feelings. The second was that he developed a new writing style, the first published fruit of which was the autobiographical masterpiece *Hadrian the Seventh* (1904). This is the inaugural use of the authorial name Fr. Rolfe, perhaps as an act of self-ordination. The prose is less baroque than in his historical works of this period and consequently more accessible. It is also satirical. He tells his own story with the same romantic turn as used in the tale of Arthur, Duke of Brittany. In the novel *Hadrian the Seventh*, George Rose, an expelled seminarian whose poverty and other tribulations rebuke the Catholic Church for failure to recognize a genuine vocation, is elected Pope as a compromise choice in a deadlocked Papal election. As Pope, Hadrian VII ends the diplomatic stalemate with Italy over the occupation of the Papal States and resolves the other European antagonisms that were to lead to World War I only a decade after the book was published. Hadrian VII dies suddenly at the hand of an anarchist, a martyr to the success of his political insight and diplomacy.

Corvo (as we may continue to call him) returned to Italy and settled in Venice in 1908, never to leave. Friends he came to distrust tried to do what they could to pay his passage home and settle his debts, but he turned on everyone who came to his aid. The prose of the works completed in the Venice years is like the prose of *Hadrian* but progressively more satirical as Corvo became progressively more paranoiac. *The Desire and Pursuit of the Whole: A Romance of Modern Venice* (published 1934) and *Nicholas Crabbe; or, The One and the Many* (published 1958) feature caricatures of everyone who had ever crossed his path, including the expatriates who gave him shelter after he was reduced to sleeping in a gondola. The satirical portraits may have interfered with the publishability of these late works, but a greater problem was the sexual content. Some early commentators were troubled by the celebration of the attractions of adolescent boys in the Toto stories. But the celebration of decadent androgyny in turn-of-the-century Venice was more troubling in the works of this late period although they are less explicit than the *Venice Letters* to Charles Masson Fox (published 1974) composed at the same time. Much more openly than the stories of a decade earlier, these last two novels combine sensuality with Corvo's control of the stylistic flourishes in his Renaissance novels, and, as a result, these last novels have an interest for contemporary readers now that time has both dimmed awareness of the targets of satire and forestalled shock about content.

Fr. Rolfe, Baron Corvo died 23 October 1913 in Venice. Corvo has a considerable cult following, perhaps traceable to the 1934 A. J. A. Symons biography *The Quest for Corvo*. Corvo's curious subject matter and checkered publication history have also given his works a special value to collectors. A major stylist of fin-de-siècle decadence, Corvo fueled his writing career with personal vendetta but also found for himself the perfect subject matter with which to create the distinctive characteristics of all three incarnations of Corvine prose.

Stories Toto Told Me includes six early stories essentially narrated in the words of the servant boy Toto.

Stories I, II, and III are narrated directly by Toto to his Master. Stories IV, V, and VI have a filtering frame narration by the Master, V and VI perhaps to justify the technical theological knowledge that these stories include. The narrative transitions of Story VI, "About One Way in Which Christians Love One Another," include a number of naturalistic representations of oral composition. At one point Toto backtracks to supply missing detail, saying, "Now I ought to have told you this," and afterwards returns to the main narrative, saying, "Now I must go to another part of the story." The frame narration serves a different purpose in Story IV, "About Beata Beatrice and the Mamma of San Pietro," than in Stories V and VI. The tale of Beatrice is a slight but engaging anecdote of the discovery by the Master of the androgynous character of Toto's beloved. It has no necessary relationship to the story that Toto then narrates and seems to exist for its own sake as a celebration of this romantic ideal of androgyny.

The character and charm of Toto are consistent. But Toto's English is perhaps implausibly good if not impossible. And in some places his knowledge of theology seems improbably complete in light of his moral naïveté in other places. For example, his recreation of Heaven relies on a childlike vision of the afterlife as a place of fun and games. In "About the Lilies of San Luigi," which is set in Heaven, Toto depicts two patron saints of adolescence laughing at a third for preferring the lilies of this world to those of the next, and God allows the two to play a trick on the third to show him that his earthly venerators do not do proper honor to his memory. This is all good, clean fun in terms of this world, but the events are set in the next world without any acknowledgment of the fundamental principle of Christianity that the Beatific Vision of the saints in Heaven makes good, clean fun irrelevant. On the other hand, in "About the Heresy of Fra Serafino" Toto's narrative turns on tracing the source of a citation in a sermon by a Franciscan preacher back through Pope Gregory the Great to St. Paul's Epistles.

The narrative structure of the stories is also a mixture of the conventional format of literate culture and the less predictable connections of folktale and myth. For example, like a fable out of Aesop, "About the Heresy of Fra Serafino" ends with structured foiling of the Jesuit antagonist who is shown up as thinking he knows more about theology than the Holy Ghost, but the story lacks the literary coda needed to explain that all the characters have misunderstood the text "No one shall be crowned unless he has contended lawfully" by taking it to mean that physical martyrdom is necessary to salvation.

"About Beata Beatrice and the Mamma of San Pietro" indicates in its very title the mixing of genres. Having in the voice of the Master exclaimed over the attractions of adolescence perhaps just so much as he thought readers could accept, Corvo has the Master snatch at a passing observation of Toto's to turn the conversation to something else: "Here I saw a chance of changing the subject, and remarked that it would be nice to know what sort of a mamma the Madonna had given to San Pietro." What follows is Toto's elaborate

fable of someone (the mother of St. Peter) so anxious
to prevent other people from an undeserved welcome
into Heaven that she loses her own chance. Beatrice
disappears from the story and from the consciousness
of the Master, whose closing remark after Toto's story
is only "I chuckled at Toto's moral reflections." On
the whole, however, *Stories Toto Told Me* is particularly
good at balancing the requirement of narrative closure
against the pose of innocence.

One indication of judicious control of style in these
stories is the way Italian vocabulary is used. Although
there is quite a bit of Italian, it never appears as central
terminology necessary to understanding the meaning
of a passage. Typically it occurs in direct address, exclamations, and colorful characterizations, the negative
implications of which can be surmised from the con-
text. On the other hand, a reader who knows Italian
will see that one character has a name that, while
plausible, actually means "Dumbbell the Parrot." And
cultural references are also manipulated to have maxi-
mum effect for those with minimum knowledge. The
Italian form of the saints' names and of various monu-
ments in Rome disguises for English readers without
the language one level of reality, but the names nevertheless provide additional atmosphere the way the
exclamations do. The people and places are, however,
real, and for those who do possess this knowledge, it
can ground in historical reality stories with a playful
and escapist surface. Some facts of this sort are that the
saints in "About the Lilies of San Luigi" are patrons of
adolescence, that the artworks mentioned in "About
Beata Beatrice and the Mamma of San Pietro" cele-

brate young men erotically, that the opera singer Lina Cavalieri was renowned for the tightness of her corsets, and that Mehemet Ali helped rebuild the Basilica of St. Paul-without-the-Walls after one of its collapses.

The prose style is the most distinctive virtue of these stories. While Corvo's historical works are famous—and justly admired—for their baroque extravagances and while his late works are interesting for their psychology and satire, the beauties of the early stories reprinted here are more subtle. Corvo is at his most transparent as a stylist in these stories.

EDMUND MILLER
Long Island University
April 7, 2008

ABOUT THE EDITOR

Edmund Miller, Chairman of the English Department at the C. W. Post Campus of Long Island University, has published a number of encyclopedia articles on Baron Corvo and a short story about him. His scholarly work includes *Drudgerie Divine: The Rhetoric of God and Man in George Herbert* and other books and articles on a wide range of authors and topics. Miller's most recent creative writing is *The Go-Go Boy Sonnets: Men of the New York Club Scene.*

Bibliography for Further Reading

Benkovitz, Miriam J. *Frederick Rolfe, Baron Corvo: A Biography*. New York: Putnam, 1977.

Cruise, Colin. "Baron Corvo and the Key to the Underworld." *The Victorian Supernatural*. Edited by Nicola Bown, Carolyn Burdett, and Pamela Thurschwell. Cambridge: Cambridge University Press, 2004. 128-148.

Ganteau, Jean-Michel. "Fantastic, but Truthful: The Ethics of Romance." *Cambridge Quarterly* 32.3 (2003): 225-238.

Gilsdorf, Jeanette W., and Nicholas A. Salerno. "Frederick W. Rolfe, Baron Corvo: An Annotated Bibliography of Writings about Him." *English Literature in Transition* 23 (1980): 3-83.

Healy, Philip. "Man Apart: Priesthood and Homosexuality at the End of the Nineteenth Century." *Masculinity and Spirituality in Victorian Culture*. Edited by Andrew Bradstock, Sean Gill, Anne Hogan, and Sue Morgan. Basingstoke: Macmillan, 2000. 100-115.

Modlish, Maureen. "Frederick William Rolfe (Baron Corvo)." *British Novelists, 1890-1929: Traditionalists*. Edited by Thomas F. Staley. Dictionary of Literary Biography. Vol. 34. Detroit: Gale, 1984. 249-254.

Parker, Jeffrey D. "Frederick William Rolfe (Baron Corvo)." *British Short-Fiction Writers, 1880-1914: The Romantic Tradition*. Edited by William F. Naufftus. Dictionary of Literary Biography. Vol. 156. Detroit: Gale, 1995. 291-300.

Symons, A. J. A. *The Quest for Corvo: An Experiment in Biography*. Introduction by Julian Symons. 1934, revised 1955. Harmondsworth: Penguin, 1966.

Weeks, Donald. *Corvo*. London: Joseph, 1971.

Woolf, Cecil. *A Bibliography of Frederick Rolfe, Baron Corvo*. 1957. Revised edition, London: Hart-Davis, 1971.

Woolf, Cecil, and Brocard Sewell, eds. *New Quests for Corvo: A Collection of Essays by Various Hands*. Introduction by Pamela Hansford Johnson. London: Icon, 1961.

Note on the Text

The text of the present edition is that of the first edition, published by John Lane at London in 1898. The original edition contained a handful of minor printer's errors, mostly with regard to the spelling of Italian words. Where it was clear that errors were the printer's, not Corvo's, they have been silently corrected for this edition.

STORIES TOTO TOLD ME

CONTENTS

Stories Toto Told Me

I

ABOUT SAN PIETRO AND SAN PAOLO

ONCE upon a time, sir, the people in Rome were building two churches; the one for San Pietro on the Monte Vaticano, and the other for San Paolo outside the walls of the city. The two saints used to spend all their spare time sitting on one of the balconies of heaven, and watching the builders; for they were both very anxious about their churches. San Pietro desired to have his church finished before that of San Paolo; and so, every night after it was dark outside, he used to leave the keys of heaven in the porch, and ask his brother, Sant'Andrea, to give an eye to the gate while he went round the corner for a minute or two. Then he would slip down to the church of San Paolo, and take to pieces the work which the builders had done during the day; and if there were any carvings, or pillars, or things of that sort which took his fancy, he would carry them away and build them into his own church, patching up the part he had taken them from so well that no one could tell the difference. And so, while the builders of the church of San Pietro made a progress which was wonderful, the builders of the church of San Paolo did not make any progress at all.

This went on for a long while, and San Paolo became more uneasy in his mind every day, and he could not take his food, and nothing gave him any pleasure. Santa Cecilia tried to amuse him with some new songs she had made; but this made him quite angry, for he said that a woman ought to learn in silence with subjection.

One day, while he was leaning over the balcony, he saw two pillars taken into his church, which were of yellow antique, most rare and precious, and had been sent from some foreign country (I do not know its name). He was altogether delighted; and he went down to the gate and asked San Pietro to be so kind as to tell him whether he had ever seen finer pillars. But San Pietro only said they were rather pretty, and then he asked San Paolo to get out of the way and let him shut the gate, in case some improper souls should sneak in.

That night, sir, when it was dark, San Pietro went and robbed those two pillars of yellow antique, and set them up in his own church. But in the morning, San Paolo, who had thought of nothing but his new pillars all through the night, said a black mass because it was shorter, and then went on to the balcony to have the pleasure of looking at his church with its beautiful pillars of yellow antique. And when he saw that they were not there he became disturbed in his mind, and he went and sat down in a shady place to consider what he should do next. After much thought, it appeared to him that he had been robbed, and as he knew that a person who has once committed a theft will continue to steal as long as he remains free, he resolved to watch his church at night, that he might discover who had stolen his pillars.

During the day the builders of the church of San Paolo put up two fresh pillars of yellow antique, and two of porphyry, and two of green antique as well. San Paolo gloated over these fine things from his seat on the balcony, for he knew them to be so beautiful that they would tempt the thief to make another raid, and then he would catch him.

After the Ave Maria, he made friends with one of the angels, who was putting on his armour in the guard-room before taking his place in the line of sentries who encircle the city of God both by day and night. These angels, sir, are a hundred cubits high, and San Paolo asked one of them, whose post was near the gate, to hide him under his wings so that he could watch for the robber without being seen. The angel said that he was most happy to oblige; for San Paolo was a Roman of Rome, and very well thought of in heaven; and when the night came on San Paolo hid in the shadow of his feathers.

Presently he saw San Pietro go out of the gate, and the light, of which the bodies of the saints are made, went with him, so that, though the earth was in darkness, San Paolo could see plainly all that he did. And he picked up the two fresh pillars of yellow antique, and the two of red porphyry, and also the two of green antique in his hand, just as you, sir, would pick up six paintbrushes; and he carried them to his own church on the Monte Vaticano and set them up there. And when he had patched up the place from which he had taken the pillars so that they could not be missed, he came back into heaven.

San Paolo met him at the gate and accused him of thieving, but San Pietro answered blusteringly that he was the Prince of the Apostles, and that he had a right to all the best pillars for his church. San Paolo replied that, once before, he had had occasion to withstand San Pietro to the face because he was to be blamed (and that was at Antioch, sir); and then high words arose, and the two saints quarrelled so loudly that the Padre Eterno, sitting on His great white throne, sent San Michele Arcangiolo to bring the disputants into His Presence.

Then San Paolo said:

"O Re dei secoli, immortale et invisibile, —The citizens of Rome are building two churches, the one for me and the other for San Pietro; and for some time I have noticed that while the builders of my church do not seem to make any progress with their work, the church of San Pietro is nearly finished. The day before yesterday (and to-day is Saturday), two pillars of yellow antique were set up in my church, most beautiful pillars, O Signor Iddio, but somebody stole them away during the night. And yesterday six pillars were set up, two of yellow antique, two of green antique, and two of porphyry. To-night I watched to see if they would be stolen; and I have seen San Pietro go down and take them to his own church on the Monte Vaticano."

Then the Padre Eterno turned to San Pietro and asked if he had anything to say.

And San Pietro answered:

"O Re del Cielo,—I have long ago learnt the lesson that it is not well to deny that which La Sua Divina Maestà knows to be true; and I acknowledge that I have taken the pillars, and many other things too, from the church of San Paolo, and have set them up in my own. Nevertheless, I desire to represent that there is no question of robbery here. O Dio Omnipotente, You have deigned to make me the Prince of the Apostolic College, the Keeper of the Keys of Heaven, and the Head of Your Church on earth, and it is not fitting that the churches which men build in my honour should be less magnificent than those which they build for San Paolo. Therefore, in taking these pillars that San Paolo makes such a paltry fuss about, I am simply within my right—a right which belongs to the dignity of the rank which lo Splendore Immortale della Sua Maestà has been graciously pleased to confer upon me."

But this defence did not content the Padre Eterno. He said that the secret method in which San Pietro worked was a proof that he knew he was doing what he ought not to do; and further, that it was not fair to the men who

were building the church of San Paolo to take
away the fine things for which they spent their
money for the honour of San Paolo. So He cau-
tioned San Pietro not to allow it to occur again.

On the next day there was a festa and the
builders did not work; but on the Monday
they placed in the church of San Paolo several
slabs of lapis lazuli and malachite; and during
the night San Pietro, who was the most bold
and daring of men, had the hardihood to take
them away and put them in his own church,
right before the very eyes of San Paolo, who
stood at the gate watching him. By the time
he returned, San Paolo had made a complaint
before the Padre Eterno; and San Pietro was
most severely spoken to, and warned that, if
he persisted in his disobedience, not even his
exalted rank, and general usefulness, and good
conduct would save him from punishment.

The following day, which was Tuesday, a
marvellous baldachino of jasper and violet
marble, being a gift from the Grand Turk, was
put up in the church of San Paolo; and at night
San Pietro went down as usual and robbed it.
For the third time San Paolo complained to
the Padre Eterno, and then all the Court of
Heaven was summoned into the Presence to
hear judgment pronounced.

The Padre Eterno said—and His Voice, sir, was like rolling thunder—that as San Pietro had been guilty of disobedience to the Divine Decree, in that, urged on by vanity, he had taken the property of San Paolo for his own church on the Monte Vaticano; and by so doing had prevented the church of San Paolo from being finished; it was an Order that, until the end of time, the great church of San Pietro in Rome should never be completed. Also, the Padre Eterno added that, as He would give no encouragement to sneaks and telltale-tits, the church of San Paolo outside the walls, though finished, should be subjected to destruction and demolition, and, as often as it was rebuilt, so often should it be destroyed.

And you know, sir, that the church of San Paolo is always being burnt down or blown up, and that the church of San Pietro has never left the builders' hands.

II

ABOUT THE LILIES OF SAN LUIGI

You know, sir, that San Sebastiano and San Pancrazio were always very friendly together. While they lived in this world, they used to get into mischief in each other's company; for they were extremely fond of playing tricks upon the pagans who were putting the Christians to death.

Then, when their turn came, they gladly suffered martyrdom; and San Pancrazio was killed by a wild beast in the Colosseo in Rome, while San Sebastiano was shot as full of arrows as a hedgehog is of prickles; and when that did not kill him he was beaten with a club until he died. And then they both went to live in heaven for ever and the day after.

Now, I must tell you what they look like, so that you may know them when you see them. First of all, you must understand that the saints in heaven are always young; that is to say, if you are old when your life in this world comes to its end, you just shut your eyes while your angel takes you to paradise, and when you open them the next minute you are there, and you have gone back to the prime of your life, and so you are for always; but if you die while you are young you do not change your age, but remain at the age at which you died. That is, if you die a saint, or a martyr, which is better, —and, of course, you can always do that if you like. And even supposing it is good for you to have a little purgatory first, if you have kept good friends with the Madonna, she will go and take you out the Saturday after you have died, and then you can go to heaven.

And your body, too, is changed, so that you cannot have any more pains or illnesses. Oh, yes, it is made of flesh, just the same to look at as this; but instead of the flesh being made of the dust of the earth, it is made of the Fire of God, and that is why wherever the saints go they are all bright like the stars.

Ah, well! San Sebastiano was eighteen years old when he went to heaven, and so he is always eighteen years old; and San Pancrazio was fourteen, and so he is always fourteen; and they are quite as cheerful and daring and mischievous as they were in this world; so that when a joke has been played upon any of the saints, they always say, "By Bacchus! there are those boys again."

There are, of course, very many boys in heaven, but now I am only telling you of these two—San Sebastiano and San Pancrazio, and the third, whose name is San Luigi; and the angel of San Sebastiano, who is called Sebastianello.

You must know that San Luigi was altogether different to San Sebastiano and San Pancrazio. Of course, he had not been a martyr like them, though he is a very great saint indeed, and I suppose it is because he has only been in heaven a little while, and is new to the place, that his manners are so stiff. He always goes about with his eyes on the ground, you know, and there is not a bit of fun in him. You see, he was a Jesuit; and there were no such things in the world for hundreds of years after San Sebastiano and San Pancrazio had been saints in heaven. When he first came, San Sebastiano and San Pancrazio thought there was another boy like themselves to join in their games; and they were quite eager to make his acquaintance, and to give him a welcome. So the moment the choir struck up the "Iste Confessor," they rushed down to the gate to offer him their friendship. San Luigi came slowly through the archway, dressed in a cassock and surplice, and carrying a lily in his hand, and his eyes were fixed upon the ground;

but when San Sebastiano and San Pancrazio, with their arms locked together, said how pleased they were to see him, he looked up at them shyly and said, "Many thanks," and then the appearance of San Sebastiano so shocked him that he blushed deeply and veiled his eyes again, and after that he kept out of their way as much as possible.

You see, sir, San Sebastiano was quite naked: indeed he had nothing about him but his halo and an arrow; for, when the pagans made a target of him, they stripped off all his clothes, and so he came to heaven like that. You can see his picture in the Duomo whenever you choose, if you do not believe me. But he was so beautiful and muscular, and straight and strong, and his flesh so white and fine, and his hair like shining gold, that no one had ever thought of him as naked before. San Luigi, however, found him perfectly dreadful; and pretended to shiver whenever he met him, which was not very often, because San Luigi spent most of his time in the chapel saying office.

San Sebastiano did consider him a little rude, perhaps, and, of course, San Pancrazio agreed with his friend; and though they were quite good-natured and unwilling to make any unpleasantness, still they could not help feeling hurt when this newcomer—and that was the worst name they ever called him—turned up his nose because their minds and their manners were more gay and free than his.

One very hot afternoon in summer the two saints went to practise their diving in a delicious pool of cool water under a waterfall; and when they were tired of that, they lay down on the bank and dangled their legs in the stream, while the sun was drying their haloes.

Presently San Luigi came creeping along with an old surplice in his hand, and he went up to San Sebastiano and offered it to him, holding his lily up before his face all the time he was speaking. San Sebastiano did not move, but lay there on the green grass, looking at San Luigi with his merry laughing eyes, and saying not a word; and San Pancrazio did the same. San Luigi repeated his offer from behind his lily, and implored San Sebastiano to put on the surplice,—just to cover up his poor legs, he said. San Sebastiano replied that he did not think there was anything amiss with his legs, which were good enough, as far as he could see, because the Padre Eterno had made them like that, and He always did all things well. Then San Luigi offered the surplice to San Pancrazio, who was also naked, because he had been bathing; but he laughed as he answered, with many thanks, that he had some very good clothes of his own, which he would put on when his body was dry; and he pointed out his beautiful tunic of white wool with a broad purple stripe down the front, and his golden bulla, and his sandals of red leather, with the pearl crescent on the toes, for he was noble, sir, and also a Roman of Rome. San Luigi said that the tunic was rather short but it was better than nothing; and then he turned to San Sebastiano and again entreated him to put on the surplice.

Presently San Sebastiano stretched out his splendid arm from the long grass where he lay, and grabbed the surplice so suddenly that San Luigi dropped down on his knees, and his lily became disarranged; and while he was picking himself up San Sebastiano rolled the surplice into a ball and tossed it over to San Pancrazio, who threw it back to him; and the two saints played ball with it quite merrily for some minutes, and all the time San Luigi was protesting that he had not brought it out for that purpose, and beseeching them not to be so frivolous. But the game amused them to such an extent that they were now running to and fro upon the bank, and taking long shots at each other. San Sebastiano had just made a particularly clever catch, but in returning the ball he over-balanced himself and tumbled splash, heels over head, into the pool. This had a bad effect on his aim, and instead of the ball going in the direction he intended—that is to say, towards San Pancrazio—it flew straight in San Luigi's face. He was still holding up his lily for a screen, and consequently it was crushed and broken, and all the blooms destroyed; and he seemed so grieved at this that the two friends—for San Sebastiano immediately swam to the side and climbed out of the pool—tried to console him by telling him that they would get him another in two winks of an eye.

But San Luigi said that was no good, because he always got his lilies off his altars down in the world, and no others would suit him; and there were none there now, because it was not his festa till to-morrow, and nobody would offer him any lilies till then.

When they heard this, San Sebastiano and San Pancrazio burst into roars of laughter, and they made such a noise that the Padre Eterno, Who was walking in the garden in the cool of the day, sent one of the cherubini from the Aureola to know what it was all about.

San Pancrazio jumped into his tunic and put his bulla round his neck, while San Sebastiano laced his sandals for him; and then the two friends stood at "Attention!" as the Suprema Maestà e Grandezza came under the trees towards them. Of course you know, sir, that San Sebastiano was in the imperial body-guard when he lived in the world, and he had taught San Pancrazio all the drill.

Then San Sebastiano looked boldly upon the Face of God, and said:

"O Signor Iddio Altissimo, we were laughing at Luigi because he will not have the lilies of Paradise, and prefers the nasty things they put upon his altars in the world."

San Luigi got quite angry at hearing his lilies called nasty; and the Padre Eterno said that the word certainly ought not to have been used unless San Sebastiano had a very good reason.

Then San Pancrazio explained, that he was sure San Sebastiano did not mean to make any reflection upon the lilies themselves, because it would not be becoming to speak against the handiwork of the Padre Eterno; but it was because the people who offered the lilies to San Luigi did not come by them in an honourable manner, that he had said they were nasty; and San Sebastiano nodded his head and said that was just it.

These words made San Luigi still more

angry; and his wrath was so righteous and unaffected, that San Sebastiano saw he was in ignorance of the dirty tricks of his clients; so he said that if the Divina Maestà would deign to allow them, he and San Pancrazio would show San Luigi where his lilies came from. The Padre Eterno was graciously pleased to grant permission, and passed on His way, for He knew San Sebastiano to be a boy whom you could trust anywhere.

Then San Sebastiano told San Luigi that if he could put up with the company of San Pancrazio he proposed they should make a little gita into the world that very night; because, as the next day was his festa, all the boys would be getting lilies for his altars; and in the meantime he invited him to come and look over the ramparts.

So the three saints went and stood upon the wall of gold; and, beneath their feet, they could see the world whirling round in space. San Sebastiano pointed out that, by midnight, they would be just above a little white town which clustered up the side of a distant mountain. He said that it was called Genzano, and that the Prince Francesco Sforza Cesarini had there a palace with the most beautiful gardens in the world, which were sure to be full of lilies at that time of year.

San Luigi made answer that he would like to say his matins and lauds, and to get his meditation ready for the morning, before they started; and he agreed to meet San Sebastiano and San Pancrazio at a little before midnight.

You know, sir, that there is no night in heaven, or rather, I should say, that it does not get dark there; and so, when San Luigi came to look for San Sebastiano and San Pancrazio, he found them in the orchard near the gate, turning a skipping-rope for Sant'Agnese and some of her friends; but San Vito and San Venanzio, being tired of playing morra, were willing to take their places at the rope, and then they were all ready to start on their journey.

San Sebastiano called his angel, Sebastianello, and told him where he wanted to go.

I ought to have let you know that the appearance of Sebastianello was exactly like that of San Sebastiano, only he did not carry an arrow, and he had wings growing out of his arms of the same colour as his body, but getting whiter towards the tips of the feathers. And then, of course, he was as big as a giant, like all the other angels—how many yards high I cannot say, because I do not exactly know.

The three saints mounted him in this manner: San Pancrazio stood on his left instep and put one arm round his leg to steady himself; and San Sebastiano stood on his right instep and put one arm round his leg to steady himself too; San Luigi also stood on the right instep of Sebastianello, close to San Sebastiano, who clasped him round the waist with his other arm. When they were ready the angel, with a downward swoop of his wings, rose from off the wall of gold, and then, spreading them out to their full extent, remained motionless and dropped gently but swiftly towards the earth.

I should tell you that they had all made themselves invisible, as the saints do when they come down into the world, except when there is some one present who is good enough to merit a vision of the gods. And when they alighted in the garden by the magnolia tree, they left the angel there, and went to sit down near the lily-beds. You understand that no one could see them, and they rested against the edge of the fountain and waited; and San Luigi took out his beads to while away the time.

Presently, three or four men came into the garden very quietly, and they stood under the shade of a blue hydrangea bush. The eldest of them appeared to be giving directions to the others, and then they separated, and went each to a different part of the garden.

"Who were those men?" asked San Luigi.

"Tell him, 'Bastiano," said San Pancrazio in a whisper.

"Gardeners," murmured San Sebastiano; "they have to stay up all the night between the twentieth and the twenty-first of June."

"And I suppose they will be going to cut the lilies for the boys who are coming to fetch them?" said San Luigi.

San Sebastiano and San Pancrazio nearly choked with laughter; and then San Sebastiano said that, if San Luigi would have the goodness to be patient, he should see what he should see.

They watched the gardeners go and hide themselves in the syringas, and for some time there was silence.

Then there came six ragamuffin boys, creeping cautiously through the darkness, and they made their way towards the lily-beds. As soon as they got there, the men in the bushes jumped out upon them with a loud yell, whereupon the boys took to their heels and fled in a different direction from that by which they had come. The men gave chase, but they ran so swiftly that they were soon out of sight. Now, as soon as they were gone, twenty or thirty more raga-muffin boys rushed noiselessly out of the darkness, and began to cut the lilies into sheaves as fast as they could. In a short time there was not one left standing, and then they made off with their spoils and disappeared.

The next minute the gardeners came back, loudly lamenting that they had failed to catch the robbers; but when they saw the beds where the lilies once stood, they called for the Madonna to have pity on them. And the chief gardener wept, for he said the Prince would surely send him to prison.

And the three saints sat still by the fountain.

San Luigi was trembling very greatly; but because he is, as you know, of such wonderful innocence, he did not understand what he had seen; and he begged his companions to explain it to him.

So San Sebastiano told him that the boys of the world were wicked little devils, and very clever, too. So they sent the six best runners first, because they knew the gardeners would be watching. And these six were to make the gardeners chase them and lead them a long dance, so that the others could come, as soon as the place was clear, and steal the lilies. All of which had been done.

And then San Luigi was very grieved; but most of all because the gardeners would lose their places. So he asked San Sebastiano if he could not do something for them.

Then San Sebastiano said that they would be very pleased and quite happy if San Luigi would show himself to them, for they were most respectable men, and pious into the bargain; neither had they sworn nor used bad words.

But San Luigi was so modest that he did not like to show himself alone, and he held out his hands, the one to San Sebastiano and the other to San Pancrazio, saying:

"My friends—if you allow me to say so— dear 'Bastiano—dear Pancrazio—who have both been so kind to me, let us all show ourselves, and then I will give them back the lilies."

So they called Sebastianello and mounted upon his insteps again; and then a silver light, more bright than the moon, beamed from them, and the gardeners saw in the midst of the blaze the great angel by the magnolia tree, and the three saints standing in front of him— San Luigi in the middle, with San Sebastiano on his right hand and San Pancrazio on his left hand, with their arms round each other. Then the gardeners fell on their knees and returned thanks for this vision; and, as the angel spread his wings and rose from the ground, San Luigi made the sign of the cross over the garden. And the men stood amazed and watched till the brightness seemed to be only a tiny star; and so the three saints went back with Sebastianello into heaven.

And, after they had disappeared, the gardeners saw that the lily-beds were full of flowers more beautiful than had ever been seen before. But when the thieves brought their stolen flowers to the Church of San Luigi in the Via Livia they were nothing but sticks and dirty weeds.

And the three saints are most friendly together now, because San Sebastiano and San Pancrazio cannot help admiring San Luigi for his strange innocence, as well as for the strange penance with which he gained his place in heaven; and they are always delighted to do anything to oblige him, because they have been longer there than he has, and understand the ways of that blessed place so well; while San Luigi carries only the lilies of Paradise now, and is never so happy as when he is choosing the best branches of golden palm for his two martyr-friends; nor is he ever shocked at San Pancrazio because he is of a gay heart, nor at San Sebastiano because he is naked and not ashamed.

How could he be ashamed, sir?

III

A CAPRICE OF THE CHERUBIM

WHEN you have the happiness, sir, to see the Padre Eterno sitting upon His throne, I can assure you that, at least, your eyes will be delighted with the sight of many splendid persons who are there also.

These, you know, are called the angels, and they are in nine rows. All these rows are in the shape of an egg with pointed ends, just like that gold ring on your finger. Those in the first row are named serafini. Those in the second row are called cherubini; and you will find their appearance quite beautiful and curious to look at. They have neither arms, nor bodies, nor legs, like the other angels, but are simply heads like those of little boys. Their eyes are as brown as the shadows on the stream, where you fished last Thursday, when the sun was shining through the trees. Their skin, if you will only believe me, has the colour and brightness of the blue jewels which la Signora Duchessa sometimes wears, and their hair waves like the sea at Ardea. They have no ears; but, in the place where the ears of a boy would be, they have wings shaped like those of a sandpiper, and blue as the sky at day-dawn. These flutter and shine for ever in regular watches in the second ring of the Glory of the Highest, and cool the perfumed air with the gentle quivering of their feathers.

Once upon a time, some of the cherubini came to hear of the pastimes with which people in the world weary themselves; and they humbly asked permission of the Padre Eterno to make a little gita down to the earth, and to have a little divel to play with next time they were off duty. And the Padre Eterno, Who always allows you to have your own way when He knows it will teach you a lesson, making the sign of the cross, said, "✠ It is allowed to you."

So the following day a very large number—I believe about ninety-five millions, but I should not like to be quite sure, because I do not exactly know—of these beautiful little blue birds of Heaven were taken by San Michele Arcangiolo down into the world, and they perched on the trees in the gardens of the Palazzo Sforza Cesarini, in that city over the lake.

San Michele Arcangiolo left them there, and made the second of his journeys into the pit of

hell. The first, you know, was after he had conquered the King of the divels in a dreadful duel
and bound him in chains and flames for ever
and the day after. As he passed along the path-
way, down the red-hot rocks, the flames of the
burning divels licked up till, meeting the cool
air of Heaven which San Michele Arcangiolo
breathed, they curved backward, and still
upward, forming a sort of triumphal arch of
yellow flame above his head.

When he arrived at the gate where hope
must be laid down, he called aloud that the
Father and King of gods and men had occasion for the services of a young imp named
Aeschmai Davi. The arch-fiend shook his chains
with rage, because he was obliged to obey; and
caused a horrible dæmon to flash into bodily
shape from a puddle of molten brimstone.

If you looked at his face or his body, you
would have thought he was a boy about fourteen years old; but his eyeballs glittered with
the red of a burning coal. If you looked at his
arms, you would have thought he was a bat,
for wings grew there of spikes and skin. Oh,
and he had nasty little horns in his hair, but it
was not hair but vipers; and from his waist to
his feet he was a he-goat, and all over he was
scarlet. It was a different scarlet to the scarlet

coat of that English soldier whom I saw once near the Porta Pia of Rome. I can only make you understand what I mean, by saying that it was the colour of the ashes of burning wood, which have been almost dead, but which you have blown up again into a fiery glow. He was of the most bad and hideous from his hoofs to his horns; and no one, whether he was a saint, or an angel, or a man like you, sir, as long as he had the protection of the Madonna, would need to be a bit afraid of him, because his nastiness was clear, and he could be seen through like a piece of glass; and in the middle of him there was his dirty dangling heart as black as ink.

San Michele Arcangiolo, who knows exactly how to deal with everybody, and especially with a *scimiotto* like this, stuck his lance into the middle of the little divel's stomach, just as Gianetta would spit a woodcock for toasting, and holding it out before him, because it is always best to see mischief in front of you, carried the writhing, wriggling little divel up into the world. The flames, as before, licked upward and around the great archangel, but never a feather was singed nor a blister came upon his whitest skin, because they could not pierce the ice of his purity; but they made the little divel kick and struggle,—just as I should, sir, if you whipped me naked with a whip of red-hot wires, instead of with the lilac twigs you do use when I am disobedient.

So they came into the Prince his garden; and having released the little divel from his uncomfortable position, San Michele Arcangiolo—who, because he commands the armies in heaven, is very fond of soldiers—went down into the city to pass a half-hour inspecting the barracks.

When the little divel found himself free, he could hardly believe his good luck, and sat for a few minutes rubbing the sparks out of his eyes, and wondering what his next torture would be. Meanwhile, the cherubini sat in the trees saying nothing, but watching with all their might, for they never had seen such a thing before.

Presently, as nothing happened to the little divel, he plucked up what small courage he had and took a sly look round. The first thing he saw was the fountain near the magnolia tree; and as the divels know very well what water is, although a rare commodity in their own country, where one drop is worth more than all the wealth the world has ever seen, he plunged head first into the basin, to cool the burning pangs which always torment him. And still the cherubini said not a word, but watched with all their eyes.

Now the basin, sir, is a deep one, as you know, because you have often dived in there yourself when the sun was in Leo. And the little divel disappeared under the water. But a moment after his head popped up, twitching with pain, amid clouds of steam and a frightful hissing; and he screamed very much and began to clamber over the edge as fast as possible.

When he got on to the grass, he jumped and skipped all over the place, and shook his wings and squeezed his hairy legs, and stroked his naked breast, and rolled about on the ground, and leaped and howled, till the cherubini found him most diverting, and laughed so much that they tumbled out of the trees, and came and fluttered round the little divel; for this was a far funnier entertainment even than that which they had promised themselves.

And the reason of it all is very easy to understand, if you will only think. You see, one of the torments that the divels and the damned have to bear is to be always disappointed; they never get their wishes fulfilled; all their plans, no matter how carefully they construct them, fall to the ground; all their arrangements are always upset at the very last moment, and everything goes by the rule of contrary. So when the wretched little creature plunged into the cold water, the heat of hell-flame boiled it, and the Breath of God made it hotter still; and so, instead of being cooled at all, the little divel got handsomely scalded.

Now, when the cherubini had had their fill of laughter, and could observe accurately this sight, which was to them so strange, they saw great patches of scalded flesh hanging in shreds and strips from his neck and sides and back and belly, and the skinny leather of his wings crinkled and warped, and the horn of his hoofs beginning to peel; and they would have felt sorry, if to grieve over a little divel had not been wrong. So they said nothing, hovering in the air around him, and looking at him with their clear eyes all the time.

The little divel looked at them too; and, being a cheeky little beast, he asked who, the hell, they were staring at.

They said that they wanted to play with him, and they desired him to do some more tricks, and to tell them merry stories, and where he came from, and what he did there, and how he liked it, and why he had that nasty black heart-shaped blotch hanging in the middle of his inside, and many other things.

And the little divel said that he had had a bad accident, and he was not going to hurt his throat by shouting to a lot of blue birds up there in the sky; and if they wanted him to answer their questions, they must come down lower, because he was in great pain.

And the cherubini wondered very much where this pain could be in which the little divel said he was, and, also, what kind of thing was this same pain: but, as they were curious and wanted to know, they descended a bit until they fluttered in a ring round and round the little divel's head.

And there they became aware of a horrible stench, and they said to one another: "He stinks—stinks of sin!" But, because they wished to be diverted, they resolved to put up with small inconveniences for a while.

Still the little divel was not satisfied; and perceiving that these would be very agreeable playmates, he tried to make a good impression. So he flopped down upon his stomach, and propped his chin up in his hands, and invited the cherubini to come and sit round him and listen to such tales as they had never heard before.

And the cherubini came a little lower, but they did not sit down.

And then other things happened.

And, suddenly, the cherubini found that they did not desire to play with this little divel any longer; and with one swoop of their wings, sounding like the strong chord you strike, sir, when you begin to play on the chitarone in the evening, they went back into Paradise; while the earth opened under the little divel, and a red flame, shaped like a hand with claws, came up and gripped and squeezed him so tightly round the waist, that his face bulged, and his eyes went out like crabs', and his breasts swelled like pumpkins, and his shoulders and arms like sausages, and his middle was like Donna Lina's, and the skin of his hairy thighs became balloons and burst, and then he was tossed back into his puddle of molten brimstone.

When the Ave rang, and this company of cherubini went on duty in the Aureola, the Padre Eterno observed, from the expression of their faces, that they had been insulted and their feelings hurt. And, when La Sua Maestà deigned to inquire the reason, they replied that the little divel, whom He had allowed them to play with, had been very rude, and they had no desire to see him any more; for they had asked him to show them funny tricks and to tell them merry stories, and where he came from, and

what he did there, how he liked it, why he had
a nasty black heart-shaped blotch dangling in
the middle of his inside, and so forth, and that
he had said he would be pleased to answer all
this and to play with them if they would come
and sit down on the grass round him; but
they had to reply that they were not able to sit
down, and the little divel had asked why not;
and they had answered politely that they had
not the wherewithal; and then the little divel
jumped up from the ground, where he was
lying with his legs a-straddling, and showed
them that he could sit down, and had turned
head over heels, and laughed and made a gibe
and a jeer of them, because he could do things
they could not do, and had also done many
other disgusting tricks before them, which had
caused them much offence; and so they were
bored and came back to Paradise.

They added that they did not desire to mix
up with that class of person again; and begged
pardon if they had seemed to prefer their own
will this time.

And the Padre Eterno smiled, and at that
Smile the light of Heaven glowed like a rain-
bow, and the music rose in a strain so beautiful
that I believe I shall die when I hear it, and He
made the sign of the cross and said: "It is well,

My children, and God bless you. Benedicat vos omnipotens Deus ✠ Pater et ✠ Filius et ✠ Spiritus Sanctus."

IV

ABOUT BEATA BEATRICE AND THE
MAMMA OF SAN PIETRO

"AH sir, don't be angry with me, because I really do love her so! What else can I do when she is as pretty as that; and always good and cheerful and patient? And when I met her last evening by the boat-house, I took her into my arms asking her to kiss me, and, sir, she did. And then I told her that I loved her dearly, and she said she loved me too. And I said that when I grew up I would marry her, and when I looked into her eyes they were full of tears, so I know she loves me; but she is ashamed because she is so poor, and her mamma such a hag. But do I mind her being poor—the little pigeon? Macché! For when I feel her soft arms round me and her breath in my hair, then I kiss her on the lips and neck and bosom, and I know it is Beatrice, her body and her soul, that I want and that I care for, not her ragged clothes."

Toto jumped off the tree trunk and stood before me, with all his lithe young figure tense and strung up, as he went on with his declamatory notices.

"Has not your excellency said that I am strong like an ox, and will it not be my joy to work hard to make my girl happy and rich and grand as the sun? Do you think that I spend what you give me at the wine-shop or the tombola? You know that I don't. Yes, I have always saved, and now I shall save more, and in a year or two I shall ask your permission to marry her. No, I don't want to go away, or to leave you. May the devil fly away with me to the pit of hell and burn me for ever with his hottest fire, if I do. Nor will Beatrice make any difference to your excellency; you need never see her, you need never even know that there is such a flower of Paradise, such an angel, living near you, if you don't wish to know it. And I can assure you that Beatrice has the greatest respect for you; and if you will only be so good and so kind as to let us make each other happy, she will be quite proud and glad to serve you as well as I do, and to help me to serve you too. And, sir, you know how fond you are of a fritto? Ah well, Beatrice can make a rigaglie so beautiful, that you will say it must have come straight from Heaven; and this I know because I have tried it myself."

He flung himself down on the ground and kissed my hands, and kissed my feet, and wept, and made me an awful scene.

I told him to get up and not be a young fool. I said that I didn't care what he did, and asked if I had ever been a brute to him, or denied him anything that was reasonable.

He swore that I was a saint, a saint from Heaven, that I always had been and always should be, because I could not help myself; and was going down on his knees again; but I stopped that; and said he had better bring me the girl, and not make me hotter than I was, with his noise.

"To tell you the truth, sir," he replied, "I was always quite sure that you would have pity upon us when you knew how very much we loved each other. And when you caught us last night, I told Beatrice that now I must let you know everything, because I was certain that, as long as I did not deceive you, and you know that I have never done so, there was nothing to be afraid of; and I told her you would without doubt like to see her to give her good counsel, because she was my friend; and she said that she would call that too much honour. Then I felt her trembling against my heart, so I kissed her for a long time, and said she must be brave like I am; and, sir, as you are so gracious as to want to see her, I have taken the liberty of bringing her, and she is here."

I had always admired the cleverness of this lad, and was not much surprised at his last announcement.

"Where?" I said.

"I put her behind that tree, sir," and he pointed to a big oak about twenty yards away. I could not help laughing at his deepness; and he took courage, I suppose, from my auspicious aspect. All sorts of clouds of hesitation, uncertainty, and doubt, moved out of his clear brown eyes, while his face set in a smile, absurd, and complacently expectant. "Shall I fetch her, sir?"

I nodded. I had had some experience of his amours before; but this was a new phase, and I thought I might as well be prepared for *anything*. He went a few paces away, and disappeared behind the oak tree. There was a little rustle of the underwood, and some kissing for a minute or two. Then he came out again, leading his companion by the hand. I said I was prepared for anything, but I confess to a little gasp at what I saw. It was not a boy and girl who approached me, but a couple of boys—apparently, at least. They came and stood beside the hammock in which I was lying. Toto, you know, was sixteen years old, a splendid, wild (*discolo*) creature, from the Abruzzi, a figure like Cellini's Perseus, skin brown, with real red blood under it, smooth as a peach, and noble as a god. He had a weakness for sticking a dead-white rose in the black waves of hair over his left ear, and the colour of that rose against his cheeks, flushed as they were now, was something to be truly thankful for. I used to make him wear white clothes, on these hot summer days down by the lake. A silk shirt with all the buttons undone and the sleeves rolled up, showing his broad brown chest and supple arms; and short breeches of the same, convenient for rowing. (He had half-a-dozen creatures like himself under his command, and their business was to carry my books, photographic and insect-hunting apparatus, and to wait upon me while I loafed the summers away in the Alban hills, or along the eastern coast.) The seeming boy, whom he had called Beatrice, looked about fourteen years old, and far more delicately dainty, even, than he was. The bold, magnificent independence of his carriage was replaced in her by one of tenderness and softness, quite as striking in its way as the other. She wore her hair in a short silky mop like Toto, and her shirt was buttoned up to the spring of her pretty throat. She was about as high as her boy's shoulder, and stood before me with her poor little knees trembling, and a rosy blush coming and going over her face. They were so exquisitely lovely, in that sun-flecked shade with the blue lake for a background, that I could not help keeping them waiting a few minutes. Such pictures as this are not to be seen every day. Presently he put his arm round her neck, and she put hers round his waist, and leaned against him a little. But he never took his eyes off mine.

"Go on, Toto," I said; "what were you going to say?"

"Ah, well, sir, you see I thought if Beatrice came to live with us—with me, I mean—it would be more convenient if she looked like the rest of us, because then she would be able to do things for you as well as we can, and people will not talk."

It struck me immediately that Toto was right again, as usual; for, upon my word, this girl of his would pass anywhere for a very pretty boy, with just the plump roundness of the Florentine Apollino, and no more.

"So I got some clean clothes of Guido's, and brought them here early this morning, and then I fetched Beatrice and put them on her, and hid her behind the tree, because I knew you would scold me about her when you came down to read the papers; and I determined to tell you everything, and to let you know that the happiness of us both was in your hands. And I only wanted you to see her like this, in order that you might know that you will not be put to any discomfort or inconvenience, if you are so kind as to allow us to love each other."

This looked right enough; but, whether or not, there was no good in being nasty-tempered just then, so I told them to be as happy as they liked, and that I would not interfere with them as long as they did not interfere with me. They both kissed my hands, and I kissed Beatrice on the forehead, and cheeks and lips, Toto looking on as proud as a white peacock. And then I told him to take her away and send her home properly dressed, and return to me in half an hour.

I could see very well that all these happenings were natural enough; and it was not a part I cared to play, to be harsh or ridiculous, or to spoil an idyll so full of charm and newness. Besides, I have reason to know, oh jolly well, the futility of interfering between the male animal and his mate.

So when Toto came back I said nothing

discouraging or *ennuyant*, beyond reminding him that he ought to make quite sure of possessing an enduring love for this girl,—a love which would make him proud to spend his life with, and for, her, and her only. I told him he was very young, which was no fault of his, and that if he would take my advice he would not be in a hurry about anything. He said that my words were the words of wisdom, and that he would obey me just as he would the Madonna del Portone in her crown of glory if she came down and told him things then and there; that he had known Beatrice since they had been babies together, and had always loved her far better than his sisters, and in a different way too, if I could only understand. Last night, when he had held her in his arms, he told her that he knew she wished him well; and felt himself so strong, and she so tender, and so tempting, that all of a minute he desired her for his own, and to give somebody a *bastonatura* of the finest for her, and to take her out of the clutches of that dirty mean old witch-cat of a mamma of hers, who never gave her any pleasure, kept her shut up whenever there was a festa, and, Saints of Heaven! sometimes beat her, simply because she envied her for being beautiful, and delicate, and bright, as a young primrose. "What a hag of a mamma it was to be cursed with, and what could the Madonna be thinking about to give such a *donnicciuola* of a mamma to his own *bellacuccia!* Not but what the Madonnina was sometimes inattentive; but then, of course, she had so many people to look after, or she could not have given such a mamma to San Pietro as she did."

Here I saw a chance of changing the subject, and remarked that it would be nice to know what sort of a mamma the Madonna had given to San Pietro.

Ah, well, sir, you must know that the mamma of San Pietro was the meanest woman that ever lived—scraping and saving all the days of her life, and keeping San Pietro and his two sisters (the nun and the other one, of whom I will tell you another time), for days together with nothing to eat except perhaps a few potato peelings and a cheese rind. As for acts of kindness and charity to her neighbours, I don't believe she knew what they were, though of course I am not certain; and whatever good San Pietro had in him, he must have picked up somewhere else. As soon as he was old enough to work he became a fisherman, as you know; because, when the Santissimo Salvatore wanted a Santo Padre to govern the Church,

He went down to the seaside and chose San
Pietro, for He knew that, as San Pietro was a
fisherman, he would be just the man to bear all
kinds of hardships, and to catch people's souls
and take them to Paradise, just as he had been
used to catch fish and take them to the market.
And so San Pietro went to Rome, and reigned
there for many years. And at last the Pagans
settled that all the Christians had to be killed.
And the Christians thought that, though they
had no objection to being killed themselves,
it would be a pity to waste a good Pope like
San Pietro, who had been chosen and given to
them by the Signor Iddio Himself. Therefore
they persuaded San Pietro to run away on a
night of the darkest, and to hide himself for a
time in a lonely place outside the gates of the
city. After he had gone a little way along the Via
Appia—and the night was very dark—he saw a
grey light on the road in front of him, and in
the light there was the Santissimo Himself; and
San Pietro was astonished, for La Sua Maestà
was walking towards Rome. And San Pietro
said: "O Master, where do you go?" And the
face of the Santissimo became very sad, and
He said: "I am going to Rome to be crucified
again." And then San Pietro knew it was not a
noble thing that he was doing, to run away on

the sly like this; because a shepherd does not leave his sheep when wolves come—at least, no shepherd worth a *baiocco*.

Then San Pietro turned round and went back himself to Rome, and was crucified with much joy between two posts in the Circus of Nero; but he would not be crucified like the Santissimo, because he wished to make amends for his weakness in trying to run away; and he begged and prayed to be crucified with his head where his feet ought to be. The Pagans said most certainly, if he liked it that way, it was all the same to them. And so San Pietro made no more ado, but simply went straight to Heaven. And, of course, when he got there his angel gave him a new cope and a tiara and his keys, and the Padre Eterno put him to look after the gate, which is a very great honour, but only his due, because he had been of such high rank when he lived in the world. Now after he had been there a little while, his mamma also left the world, and was not allowed to come into Paradise, but because of her meanness she was sent to hell. San Pietro did not like this at all, and when some of the other saints chaffed him about it he used to grow angry. At last he went to the Padre Eterno, saying that it was by no means suitable that a man of his quality should be disgraced in this way; and the Padre Eterno, Who is so good, so full of pity and of mercy that He would do anything to oblige you if it is for the health of your soul, said He was sorry for San Pietro, and He quite understood his position. He suggested that perhaps the case of San Pietro's mamma had been decided hurriedly, and He ordered her Angel-guardian to bring the book in which had been written down all the deeds of her life, good or bad.

"Now," said the Padre Eterno, "We will go carefully through this book, and, if We can find only one good deed that she has done, We will add to that the merits of Our Son and of hers, so that she may be delivered from eternal torments."

Then the Angel read out of the book, and it was found that, in the whole of her life, she had only done one good deed; for a poor starving beggar-woman had once asked her, per l'Amore di Dio, to give her some food; and she had thrown her the top of an onion which she was peeling for her own supper.

And the Padre Eterno instructed the Angel-guardian of San Pietro's mamma to take that onion-top, and to go and hold it over the pit of hell, so that if, by chance, she should boil up with the other damned souls to the top of that stew, she might grasp the onion-top and by it be dragged up to Heaven.

The Angel did as he was commanded and hovered in the air over the pit of hell, holding out the onion-top in his hand; and the furnace flamed, and the burning souls boiled and writhed like *pasta* in a copper pot, and presently San Pietro's mamma came up thrusting out her hands in anguish, and when she saw the onion-top she gripped it, for she was a very covetous woman, and the Angel began to rise into the air, carrying her up towards Heaven.

Now when the other damned souls saw that San Pietro's mamma was leaving them, they also desired to escape, and they hung on to the skirts of her gown, hoping to be delivered from their pain; and still the Angel rose, and San Pietro's mother held the onion-top, and many tortured souls hung on to her skirts, and others to the feet of those, and again others on to them, and you would surely have thought that hell was going to be emptied straight away. And still the Angel rose higher, and the long stream of people all hanging to the onion-top rose too, nor was the onion-top too weak to bear the strain: so great is the virtue of one good deed. But when San Pietro's mamma became aware of what was going on, and of the numbers who were escaping from hell along with her, she did not like it: and, because she was a nasty selfish and cantankerous woman, she kicked and struggled, and took the onion-top in her teeth, so that she might use her hands to beat off those who were hanging to her skirts. And she fought so violently that she bit through the onion-top, and tumbled back once more into hell flame.

"So you see, sir, that it is sure to be to your own advantage if you are kind to other people and let them have their own way, so long as they don't interfere with you."

I chuckled at Toto's moral reflections.

V

ABOUT THE HERESY OF FRA SERAFICO

O NE of Toto's brothers was called Nicola, and he was going to be a priest. He was nineteen years old, and very like Toto in appearance, with this notable difference—there was no light in his eyes. In manner, he was a curious, gaunt, awkward, unworldly creature; absolutely the opposite of Toto, who had the charm and freedom of a young savage on the loose. I don't know why the clergy, for whom I entertain the highest respect, of course, should always slink along by the wall, expressing by the cringing obsequiousness of their carriage that they would take it as a favour for some one to kick them, but such is the case. I used to see this Nicola sneaking about during his summer vacation, but I don't think I ever spoke to him except when he came to say "How do you do?" and "Good-bye." One morning, soon after his arrival, I asked Toto what was the matter with his brother; for he looked even more caged, humpty-backed, and slouching, more utterly miserable and crushed, than usual. "'Cola, sir,"

he said, "you must know, has a very feeling
heart; and if he meets with any little misfor-
tune it is a much more serious thing to him
than it would be to me. I, of course, would say
that it didn't matter, and look for something
else to amuse me; but 'Cola will think over his
grief so much till it seems far greater than it
really is; and he will not be able to eat his food
or take any interest in anything, and wish he
was dead or that he had never given himself the
annoyance of being born. And I suppose, now,
he has had some little trouble in his college—
dropped his garter, perhaps, and let his stock-
ing down when out with the camerata in the
street, and he has thought about it so much
that he believes he has committed a sin against
the sixth commandment, by an indecent expo-
sure of his person. But, if I have your leave, I
will ask him, for I can see him saying his beads
behind the Emissario."

Toto ran away, and I took a little nap.

When I awoke, he was coming down the
steps, holding a rhubarb leaf over his head. "I
am sure you will be much amused, sir, when
I tell you what is the matter with 'Cola," he
said. "I made him very angry with me because
I could not help laughing at him; and he said
that I should certainly burn for making a mock

of the clergy—clergy, indeed, and he only a sub-deacon, and I his brother who know all about him, and everything he ever did! And Geltruda, too! For my part, I am sure it is a gift straight from Heaven to be a priest, because I remember that 'Cola used to be quite as fond of enjoying himself as I am, but since he went to the Seminario he will not look at a petti-coat—that is to say, the face that belongs to it, for it is only the petticoats he does look at. Have I not seen my little mother cry when he came home, because he only put his lips to her hand—and they didn't touch it—as if she were la Signora Duchessa, instead of the mother who wished to take him in her arms? But his dolour now, sir, is this. You must know that at the Seminario, you have to preach to the other chierichetti in the refectory, during supper. This is to give you practice in delivering sermons. And after you have preached, you go to your place; and, if it is necessary to make any remarks upon what you have said, the profes-sors tell you all they think. Well, it was 'Cola's turn to preach the night before he came home, and he says that it was a sermon which he had taken all his life to write. He had learnt it by heart; and on arriving in the pulpit he repeated it, moving his hands and his body in a manner which he had practised before his mirror, without making a single mistake. When he had finished, the rector paid him compliments, and two or three of the other professors did the same. But when it came to the turn of the decano, who is the senior student, he said that the college ought to be very proud of having produced an abatino so clever as to be able, in his first sermon, to invent and proclaim sixteen new and hitherto unheard-of heresies. And 'Cola, instead of feeling a fine rage against this nasty, jealous prig, with his mocking tongue, takes all the blame to himself and is making himself wretched. I told him that there was no difficulty about heresies, if that was what he wanted, because I think that to do wrong is as easy as eating, and that the difficulty is to keep straight. But he says he is a miserable sinner, and that it is all his fault, for he cannot have perfectly corresponded with his vocation. Why, as for heresy, sir, I will tell you how a friar in Rome was accused of preaching heresy, and then you will know that it is not always the being accused of inventing heresies that makes you guilty of that same.

Ah, well, formerly there lived in Rome a certain friar called Fra Serafico. When he had lived in the world he was of the Princes of

Monte Corvino, but at about the age of 'Cola
he astonished everybody by giving up his rank
and his riches and his state, and becoming a
son of San Francesco. Now the fraticelli of
his convent were not quite able to understand
why a young man who had his advantages,
should give them up as he did, and prefer a
shaved head and naked feet and to be a beggar.
And Fra Serafico, though he had the best will
in the world, did not make a good impression
on the other friars, because his manners were
different to theirs. He felt miserable without a
pocket-handkerchief for his nose. And it was
some time before the superiors became certain that he had a true vocation, for he went
about his duties with diligence and humility,
feeling so shy, because the things around him
were so strange, that he gained for himself,
amongst the other novices, the nickname of
'Dumbtongue.'

And this went on until he had finished his
probation, and taken the habit and the vows.

One day after this, the Superior, in order to
give him a good humiliation, told him to pre-
pare to preach a sermon before the convent
at the chapter that afternoon. Fra Serafico
received this command in silence, and, having
kissed the ground before the Fra Guardiano,

he went away to his cell, and when the after-noon came he stood up to preach.

Then, sir, a very curious thing happened, for Fra Serafico preached, and while he preached the faces of the other friars became set in a glare of astonishment, and the eyes of the Fra Guardiano were almost starting out of his head by the time the sermon was finished. Then there was silence for a little while, and the friars looked at one another and nodded. It seems that they had been entertaining an angel unawares, for this Dumbtongue, as they called him, had turned out to be a perfect Golden-mouth. And the friars were more than glad; for, though they were all good men and very holy, they had no great preacher among them at the time, and they thought it was a shame that an order, whose business was to preach, should have no man who could preach well, and at last they saw a way out of the difficulty: 'For surely,' they said, 'this Serafico speaks the words of San Paolo himself, with the tongue of an angel.' After this he gave fervorini daily in the convent church, till all the city was filled with his fame, and at last he was named by Papa Silvio to preach the Lent in the Church of San Carlo al Corso.

Of course you know very well, sir, that the

devil is always disgusted to see the works of God going on as easily water running out of a turned-on tap, and you know also that when a good work seems to be thriving at its best, then is the time the devil chooses to try to upset it. And so he went to a little Jesuit called Padre Tonto Pappagallo—and, of course, I need not tell you that the Jesuits are not what you might call friendly to the Franciscans—and he suggested to him the evil thought, that it was a bad thing for the Jesuits to be beaten in preaching by the Franciscans, and what a score it would be if a Jesuit were to have the honour of catching Fra Serafico in the act of preaching heresy. Padre Tonto, it happened, had made a bad meditation that morning, having allowed his eyes to fix themselves upon some of the stone angels who were dangling their beautiful white legs over the arches round the apsis, and his thoughts to wander from his meditation to those things, which every good priest flies from with as much haste as he would fly from the foul fiend appearing in person. And so his mind was just like a fertile field; and when the devil popped in his suggestion, the seed immediately took root, and before the morning was over it had burst into blossom, for this Padre Tonto cut off to the Church of San Carlo to hear the great preacher; and when he saw the vast multitude all so intent upon those golden words that if an earthquake had happened then and there I believe no one would have even blinked, and when he heard the sighs from the breasts of wicked men, and saw the tears rain down on women's cheeks, he envied Fra Serafico the power to do these things; and so he began to listen to the sermon that he might catch the preacher preaching heresy. Now, of course, while he was staring about, he had not paid attention to the words of gold, and the first sentence that caught his ear when he did begin, indeed, to listen was this, 'No one shall be crowned unless he has contended lawfully.'

Padre Tonto jumped up and ran out of the church. He was delighted, for he had heard a heresy straight away. 'No one shall be crowned,' he said, 'that is, of course, with the crown of glory which the saints in heaven wear for ever —unless he has contended lawfully—that is to say, as the martyrs did in the Colosseo. Pr-r-r-r-r-r, my dear Serafico! And what, then, becomes of all the holy bishops and confessors, and of the virgins and penitents and widows whom Holy Church has numbered with the saints? These were not martyrs, nor did they fight with beasts, like San Paolo' (and I cannot tell you the place, sir). 'If I were Pope, Seraficone mio, I should burn your body in the Campo di Fiore to-morrow morning, and your soul in hell for ever and the day after.' And saying these words and all sorts of other things like them, he ran away to the Sant'Uffizio and made a mischief with much diligence.

Now Padre Tonto had a very good reputation and was exceedingly well thought of in Rome. Moreover, the accusation he made appeared to be well founded. So Fra Serafico was sent for, and the question was put to him, 'Did you or did you not, in your sermon preached in the Church of San Carlo al Corso on the second Monday in Lent, say, "No one shall be crowned unless he has contended lawfully?"' And Fra Serafico replied that his questioner, who was the Grand Inquisitor himself, spoke like a book with large letters and clasps of silver, for without a doubt he had used those very words. The Grand Inquisitor remarked that confession of wrong done was always good for the soul: and he pointed out to Fra Serafico the dreadful heresy of which he had been guilty in uttering words which, if they meant anything at all, meant this, *That it was impossible to get to Heaven unless you suffered martyrdom.* And he told Fra Serafico, that as he had made his heresy public

by preaching it to all Rome, it would be necessary to make amends also in the place of
his crime, or else to let himself be burnt with
fire in the Campo di Fiore on the next public
holiday, both to atone for the sin, and in order
to encourage other people who might feel it
their business to preach heresy as he had done.
And Fra Serafico answered that he wished to
live and die a good and obedient son of Holy
Mother Church, and to submit his judgment in
all things to hers; therefore, it would give him
much joy to make public amends for his heresy
at any time or place which his eminence, in his
wisdom, might be pleased to appoint.

The next day the people of Rome were
called by proclamation to the Church of San
Carlo al Corso to see Fra Serafico's humiliation; and because he was such a celebrated
man there came together all the noblest and
most distinguished persons in the city. Papa
Silvio sat upon the throne with the Princes
Colonna and Orsini on his right hand and on
his left. All around there were fifty scarlet cardinals, bishops by the score in purple and green,
friars grey, friars white, friars black, monks by
the hundred, and princes and common people
like raindrops. And when they had all taken
their places, Fra Serafico entered, between

two officers of the Sant'Uffizio with their faces covered in the usual manner; and first he prostrated himself before the Maestà in the tabernacle, and then at the feet of Papa Silvio, then he bowed from the waist to the Sacred College and the prelates, and from the shoulders to the rest; and then he was led into the pulpit from which he had proclaimed his heresy. There he began to speak, using these words: 'Most Holy Father, most eminent and most reverend lords, my reverend brethren, most illustrious princes, my dear children in Jesus Christ. I am brought here today on account of the vile and deadly heresy, which I am accused of preaching from this pulpit on the first Monday in Lent. That heresy is contained in the following words: "No one shall be crowned unless he has contended lawfully." I freely confess, acknowledge, and say, that I did, in real truth, use those words. But before I proceed to abjure the heresy contained in them, and to express with tears my penitence for the crime I have committed, I crave, my beloved children in Jesus Christ, most illustrious princes, my reverend brethren, most eminent and most reverend lords, and, prostrate at your feet, most Holy Father, indulgence for a few moments while I relate a dream and a vision which came to me during the night just past, which I spent for the good of my soul upon the tender bosom of the Sant'Uffizio.' Fra Serafico's face, as he spoke, beamed with a beauty so unearthly, his manner was so gracious, and the music of his golden voice so entrancing, that Papa Silvio, making the sign of the cross, granted him the favour he had asked.

The friar went on: 'In my dream it appeared to me that I was standing before the bar of the Eternal Judge; and that there I was accused by a certain Jesuit named Padre Tonto Pappagallo of having preached heresy on the first Monday in Lent, in the Church of San Carlo al Corso, using these words: "No one shall be crowned unless he has contended lawfully." And while I waited there, Beato Padre Francesco himself came and stood beside me. And the Judge of all men looked upon me with wrath and anger, asking whether I confessed my crime; and I, wretched man that I am, in the presence of Him who knows all things, even the inmost secrets of the heart, could do nothing else but acknowledge that it was even so. Then the Padre Eterno, who, though terrible beyond all one can conceive to evil-doers, is of a justice so clear, so fine, and straight, that the crystal of earth becomes as dark as mud, the keenness of a diamond as blunt granite, and the shortest distance between two points as crooked as the curves in a serpent's tail—this just Judge, I say, asked me, who am but a worm of the earth, whether I had anything to allege in excuse for my crime.

'And I, covered with confusion as with a garment, because of my many sins, replied, "O Clementissimo Signor Iddio, I have confessed my crime; and in excuse I can only say that when I was preparing my sermon, I took those words from the writings of San Gregorio."

'The Judge of all men ordered my angel to write this down, and deigned to ask whether I could say in what part of the writings of San Gregorio this heresy could be found. "O Padre Celeste Iddio," I replied, "the heresy will be found in the 37th Homily of San Gregorio on the 14th chapter of the Gospel of San Luca." Then I covered my face with my hands and waited for my dreadful sentence; but Beato Padre Francesco comforted me, and patted my shoulder with his hand, all shining with the sacred stigmata; and the Padre Eterno, speaking in a mild voice to the Court of Heaven, said, "My children, this little brother has been accused of preaching a heresy, and this heresy is said to have been taken from the

writings of San Gregorio. In this case, you will
perceive that it is not Our little brother who is
a heretic, but San Gregorio, who will therefore
have the goodness to place himself at the bar,
for We are determined to search this matter to
its remotest end." Then San Gregorio was led
by his Angel-guardian from his throne among
the Doctors of the Church, and came down to
the bar and stood beside me and Beato Padre
Francesco, who whispered in my ear, "Cheer
up, little brother, and hope for the best!" And
the Padre Eterno said, "San Gregorio, this little
brother has been accused before Us, that on the
first Monday in Lent, in the Church of San Carlo
al Corso, he preached heresy in the following
words: 'No one shall be crowned unless he has
contended lawfully.' We have examined him,
and he alleges that he has taken these words
from the 37th Homily, which you have written
upon the 14th chapter of the Gospel of San
Luca. We demand, therefore, that you should
say, first, whether you acknowledge yourself to
have written these words; and secondly, if you
have done so, what excuse you have to offer?"
And San Gregorio opened the book of his writings which, of course, he always carries with
him, and turned the pages with an anxious
finger. Presently he looked up with a smile into

the Face of God and said, "O Dio, Padre delle
misericordie, our little brother has spoken the
truth, for I have found the passage, and when
I have read it, You will find the answer to both
questions which Your Condescension has put
me." So San Gregorio read from his writings
these words, "But we cannot arrive at the great
reward unless through great labours: where-
fore, that most excellent preacher, San Paolo,
says, 'No one shall be crowned unless he has
contended lawfully.' The greatness of rewards,
therefore, may delight the mind, but does
not take away the obligation of first fighting
for it." "Hm-m-m-m," said the Padre Eterno,
"this begins to grow interesting; for it seems,
my children, that our little brother here has
quoted his heresy from San Gregorio, and that
San Gregorio in his turn quoted it from San
Paolo, upon whom, therefore, the responsi-
bility seems to rest. Call San Paolo."

'So seven archangels blew their trumpets
and summoned San Paolo, who was attending
a meeting of the Apostolic College, and when
he came into Court his Angel-guardian led him
to the bar, where he took his place by the side
of San Gregorio' (the man who made them
Christians in England, sir, and the chant, sir,
and saw San Michele Arcangiolo on the top of

the Mola), 'of Beato Padre Francesco, and of my wretched self. "Now, San Paolo," said the Padre Eterno, "We have here a little grey friar who has been accused of preaching heresy on the first Monday in Lent, in the Church of San Carlo al Corso, in these words, 'No one shall be crowned unless he has contended lawfully.' And he has informed Us that he quoted these words from San Gregorio's 37th Homily on the 14th chapter of the Gospel of San Luca. We have examined San Gregorio, and he has pointed out to Us that he did indeed use these words, as Our little brother has said; but San Gregorio also alleges that they are not his own words, but yours. The Court, therefore, would like to know whether San Gregorio's statement is true." Then San Paolo's Angel-guardian handed to him the book which contained all the letters he had written, and after he had refreshed his memory with this, the great apostle replied, "O Principio di ogni cosa, there is no doubt that both our little brother and San Gregorio are right, for I find in my second letter to San Timoteo, chapter ii. verse 5, the following words: 'And if a man also strive for masteries, yet is he not crowned except he contend lawfully.'" "Well!" said the Padre Eterno, "this is a very shocking state of things that you, San Paolo, should publish heresies in this manner, and lead men of all ages into error! San Gregorio, taking the statement on your authority, preaches heresy in his time, and a thousand years after, our little brother, innocently thinking that men of such eminence as the Apostle of the Gentiles and the Apostle of England are of good authority, preaches the same heresy. You see now that it is impossible to know what the end of a lie will be when once it has been started on its course." "But hear me," said San Paolo, who was a very bold man, "for I venture to submit to La Sua Maestà that the second letter which I wrote to San Timoteo has been placed by Your Church on earth on the list of the Canonical Books, and this means that when I wrote that letter I was inspired by the Third Person of the Maestà Coeterna dell'Adorabile Trinità and that therefore I was divinely protected from teaching error in any shape or form!" "Of course it does," replied the Padre Eterno. "The words that you have written, San Paolo, in your second letter to San Timoteo, are not the words of a man, but the Words of God Himself, and the matter amounts to this, that our little brother here, who took the words from San Gregorio, who took them from you, who were divinely inspired to write them, has not been guilty of heresy at all, unless God Himself can err. And who," continued the Padre Eterno, with indignation, "We should like to know, is the ruffian who has taken up Our time with this ridiculous and baseless charge against Our little brother?" Somebody said that it was a Jesuit named Padre Tonto Pappagallo, at which the Padre Eterno sniffed and said, "A Jesuit! and what, in the name of goodness, is that?"

'So the Madonna whispered that it was a son of Sant'Ignazio of Loyola. "Where is Sant'Ignazio of Loyola?" said the Padre Eterno. Now Sant'Ignazio, who had seen the way things were going, and what a contemptible spectacle his son was presenting, had hidden himself behind a bush and was pretending to say his office. But he was soon found and brought into Court, and the Padre Eterno asked him what he meant by allowing his spiritual children to act in this way. And Sant'Ignazio only groaned and said, "O Potenza Infinita, all my life long I tried to teach them to mind their own business, but in fact I have altogether failed to make them listen to me."

'That was my dream, Most Holy Father, most eminent and most reverend lords, my reverend brethren, most illustrious princes, my beloved children in Jesus Christ; and since you have been so gracious as to listen, I will no longer delay my recantation of the heresy of which I am accused of having preached on the first Monday in Lent, in the Church of San Carlo al Corso.'

But Papa Silvio arose from his throne and the cardinals, and the bishops, and the princes, and the people, and the people, and they all cried in a loud voice, 'Evviva, evviva, Bocca d'Oro, evviva, evviva.'"

VI

ABOUT ONE WAY IN WHICH
CHRISTIANS LOVE ONE ANOTHER

"YES," I said, "that's a very good story, Toto. And now I want to know where you learnt it."

"Well, sir," he replied, "it was told to me by Fra Leone of the Cappuccini. Not that I wish you to think the Cappuccini and Franciscans to be the same, not at all. But, of course, you know better than that, and it is like their impertinence of bronze to pretend that they are, as they do, for the Cappuccini were not even heard of for hundreds of years after San Francesco founded his Order of Little Brothers. And the reason why they came to be made was only because of the vain man Simon Something-or-other, who gave more thought to his clothes than was good for his soul, and found that the sleeves which were good enough for San Francesco, and the round tippet which that heavenly saint wore did not suit his style of beauty, and so he made himself a brown habit instead of a grey one, with plain sleeves to show the shape of his arms, and no pockets in them, and a tippet not round but pointed like the piece of flesh there is between my shoulders. And then, because there are always plenty of men ready to run after something new, he got together so many followers who wished to dress themselves like him, that the Santo Padre preferred to give them permission to have their own way, rather than cause them to become rebels against our Holy Mother the Church, by making it difficult for them to be obedient; because the matter had really no importance to speak of."

I said that I knew all about that, but that I didn't believe that religious men, whether they were Franciscans, or sham ones like the Cappuccini, or even Jesuits, would show such jealousy and envy of each other as appeared in the story of Fra Serafico.

"And there," said Toto, "I can assure you that you are altogether wrong. I may tell you that in every religious order there are two kinds of men—the saints and the sinners; and of course, the saints always love each other as Francesco and Domenico did; and, by contrary, having submitted themselves to the infernal dragon who always drives all love out of the hearts of his slaves and inflames them with the undying fire of envy, the sinners hate each other with a hatred like the poison of vipers, and occupy themselves with all kinds of schemes by which they may bring discredit upon their enemies, the sinners of other orders. Why, I will tell you a tale which is quite true, because I have seen it, of how some Cappuccini—and you will not ask me to say where their convent is—have done a deed by which much shame will some day be brought upon a house of Jesuits who live in their neighbourhood.

Well, then, there was a convent of Cappuccini, and outside the grounds of the convent there was a small house in which I lived with my father and my mother and my brothers and sisters, and it was a very lonely place. And about as far off as it would take you to say five Paters, and five Aves, and five Glorias, there was another house, and there were perhaps three or four cottages in sight, and that is all, so it was a very lonely place. But six miles away there was a large college of Jesuits, up in the hills, and when a Jesuit died it was the custom to bury him in the churchyard of the Cappuccini. Now there was a man who came to live in the other house, and he was not an old man nor a young man, but just between the two, and because he felt lonely he used to pay attentions to all the ladies who came in his way when

visiting this celebrated convent of Cappuccini; and our difficulty was to know which one
he was going to marry. And there was one in
particular who appeared to these Cappuccini
to be the one that he ought to marry, but her
home was far away in a large town; and so one
of the friars wrote to her parish priest to ask
what ought to be done; and the parish priest
replied: 'Yes, you must get her married as soon
as possible'; and soon after that the respectable
man married her and brought her to the house
in the lonely place that I am telling you about.
And they lived there very quietly for a little
while, and then his business called the respectable man away from his house for a few weeks.
So he went, and his wife remained at home;
and there was no one in the house besides her
but a woman, her servant.

And presently, in the middle of one night,
there was a knocking at the door of the small
house where I lived with my father and my
mother and my brothers and my sisters, and
I heard this knocking because that night I was
going to enjoy myself in the orchard of the
Cappuccini. So I came downstairs in my shirt
only; and, because I wished to keep secret what
I was going to do, I left my shirt rolled up in a
bundle under the seat in the porch, and I will

tell you why: I thought of two things; the first thing was that it was a very rainy night, and if my mother found in the morning that my shirt was wet, she would guess I had been up to mischief, and, having told my father, I should have nothing but stick for breakfast; and the second thing was that if some Cappuccino should be persuaded by an uneasy devil to look out of his window to see a naked boy running about in the orchard or in the churchyard, he would say to himself that it was just a poor soul escaping from purgatory, and then, having repeated a De Profundis, he would go back to his bed. So just as I was creeping across the yard with the warm rain pouring in torrents over my body, there came this banging on the door of my house, and I skipped behind a tree and waited. Then my father opened the window of his room upstairs, demanding what was the matter, and the voice of the servant of the respectable man, replied that la Signora Pucci had suddenly been taken very ill, and that if my mother was a Christian woman she would come to her assistance. This servant spoke with a very thick voice; and as I did not think I was going to be amused if I stayed behind my tree, I ran away and enjoyed myself enough with the peaches belonging to these Cappuccini.

When I came home I dried myself with a cloth, took my shirt from under the seat in the porch, and went to bed again. And in the morning when I awoke there was no one to give us our breakfast; for my father was gone to his work, and my mother to the assistance of the wife of the respectable man; so I was thankful enough that I had made so many good meals during the night. All that day, and all the next night, and the day after, was my mother away from her home; and I need not tell you that I began to think that something very strange was happening, of which I ought to know; so I waited here, and I waited there, and I put a question of one kind to this, and a question of another kind to that, and during the night, after my father had seen me go to bed, I got up again, left my shirt in the porch as before, not because it was raining now, but because I liked it, as well as for the other reason, and I wandered about quite naked and happy and free" (here he tossed his arms and wriggled all over in an indescribable manner), "dodging behind trees and bushes, from my father's house to the house of the respectable man, and to the churchyard of the convent of the Cappuccini; and during that night I saw many curious things; and these, with the answers which were given to the questions I had been asking, and other odds and ends, which I either knew, or had seen with my eyes, made me able to know exactly what this mystery was.

"Now I ought to have told you this, that a week before, a priest from the Jesuit college of which I have already spoken had been buried in the convent churchyard; also he was the confessor of the wife of the respectable man, and a priest whom she held in the very greatest honour, and he was called Padre Guilhelmo Siretto. He was a saint indeed whom everybody venerated, for the Signor Iddio had made him live sixty-seven years in order that he might add to the many good deeds which in his long life he had done. I should like you to remember this, because now I must go to another part of the story.

After the servant of the respectable man had told my father that her mistress was ill, my mother arose from her bed and went at once to the house of the sick person. Arrived there, she found la Signora Pucci fallen upon the floor in great pain; and, being a woman herself, she knew with one stroke of her eye what was the matter.

Now the servant of the respectable man, who had accompanied my mother, was drunk, and so useless. Therefore my mother, who is the best of all women living, made la Signora Pucci as comfortable as she could at that time, went into the stable, put the horse into the cart, and, having driven for three miles to the nearest town, brought a doctor back with her as the day was breaking.

The sick woman was put to bed, and the doctor gave my mother directions as to what was to be done during his absence: for he said he must go home now to finish his night's rest, and in the morning he had his patients to see, but in the afternoon he would come again, and that then, perhaps, something would happen. But my mother told him that she would on no account consent to be left alone in the house with la Signora Pucci, because she perceived that something most astonishing was to happen. The doctor replied that he would not stay, because he could not; and that if my mother was not there to assist the sick woman in her trouble, she might die. But my mother would by no means be persuaded, and in the end she conquered; and the doctor stayed, and they waited all through the night, and the next morning at noon there came a new baby into that house; and la Signora Pucci was so astonished that she really nearly died, and as for the baby, he did die after a half-hour of this world.

Then the sick woman became mad, and cried in delirium that she would not have it known to the respectable man, her husband, that a new baby had come into that house; so my mother went for the Fra Guardiano of these Cappuccini, telling him all that she knew, how she had baptized the baby herself, by the name Angelo, seeing that he was at the point of death, and that therefore he must be buried in the churchyard; and how his mother, la Signora Pucci, demanded that this should be done secretly, and that the grave should be made with Padre Guilhelmo, of whom I have told you before, who was a saint that any person might be glad to be buried with. Upon which the Fra Guardiano replied that this was as easy as eating; and he directed my mother, having put the dead baby into a box, to take the box under her cloak at midnight to the grave of Padre Guilhelmo. So she did as she was told, putting the dead baby Angelo into a wooden box in which rice had been, and cutting a cross upon the lid so that San Michele Arcangiolo should know there was a Christian inside; and at midnight she was there at the grave of Padre Guilhelmo. And, of course, I need not tell you that there was a naked boy hidden in a cedar tree, over her head, lying flat upon his face upon a thick branch which he held between his thighs and with his arms, and looking right down upon the grave. Then there came out of the convent Fra Giovannone, Fra Lorenzo, Fra Sebastiano, and Fra Guilhelmo. And if I had not remembered that a naked boy in a cedar-tree was not one of the things which you are unable to do without at a midnight funeral, I should have laughed, because these friars, coming out of their convent without candles, fell over the crosses on the graves, and said things which friars do not say in their offices. They brought two spades and a bucket of holy water, and when they came to the grave of the Jesuit Padre, Fra Sebastiano and Fra Guilhelmo dug about three feet of a hole there; then my mother gave them the box from under her cloak, and they put it in the earth; and having sprinkled it with holy water, they covered it up, made the grave look as it had looked before, as best they could in that dim light, and then returned to their convent, all the time saying no word aloud.

Then my mother went back to the house of la Signora Pucci, and a boy without clothes fol-lowed her there. For one hour after I ran back-wards and forwards secretly from the convent to the house of the respectable man, but finding that nothing else happened I went to my bed.

About the end of the day after this my mother returned to her house, and said that the doctor had brought a nurse to la Signora Pucci, and that the respectable man her husband also was coming back, so there was nothing more for her to do. Then she swooned with weariness, for she was tired to death; but having rested some days while I and my sisters and my brothers kept the house clean and tidy, she recovered herself.

And that is all the tale, sir.

And I think you will see that these Cappuccini, unless indeed they are entirely fools of the most stupid, and that they may be, have been urged on by envy of the Jesuit fathers to lay the beginnings of a plot which some day will cause a great scandal. You must see that they could not help the coming of the new baby Angelo to the house of the respectable man, and it is not for that that I blame them. You must see that when the new baby Angelo had come, and died a Christian, there was nothing else for them to do but to bury him in their churchyard; and that secretly, to defend la Signora Pucci from shame; and after all you must see that there are yards and yards and yards of ground in that churchyard where this dead Christian baby Angelo could be buried by himself secretly, and that it is simply abominable to have put him into the grave of a Jesuit, which, being opened, as it may at any time—God knows when or why, but it is quite likely—will bring a great dishonour and a foul blot upon the sons of Sant'Ignazio of Loyola."

I said that I saw.

Thus ended the sixth of the nine and forty Stories Toto Told Me: wherein have been contained high and great matters concerning the noble army of martyrs and all the company of heaven with other divers legends histories and acts as all along hereafore is made mention. Which works I have so far written down for the first time at the commandment and request of my special patron John Lane, and have finished at Corvicastra in Aria on the feast of the good thief Saint Dismas the year of Our Lord m viijc xc viij and the lx i year of the reign of Queen Victoria. By me Baron Corvo. Printed for John Lane by John Wilson & Son at the University Press Cambridge Mass., in August m viijc xc viij

NOTES

I. ABOUT SAN PIETRO AND SAN PAOLO

5   *San Pietro on the Monte Vaticano*: St. Peter's Basilica on Vatican Hill in Rome, the seat of the Papacy.

5   *San Paolo outside the walls of the city*: The Basilica of St. Paul was erected originally by Constantine I (272-337), the first Christian Emperor, over what was believed to be the burial place of St. Paul the Apostle.

5   *Sant'Andrea*: St. Andrew the Apostle was the brother of St. Peter (John 1:40).

6   *Santa Cecilia*: St. Cecilia, the patron saint of music, was a married virgin who heard Jesus singing in her heart as her wedding music played.

6   *yellow antique*: Wood treated with the specific finish polish of this name.

7   *black mass*: Not the sacrilege of the Witches' Sabbath but an abbreviated version of the mass without consecration, formerly the norm for the Good Friday services.

9   *San Paolo . . . had had occasion to withstand San Pietro . . . at Antioch*: In Galatians 2:11 St. Paul describes talking St. Peter (regarded as successively Bishop of Jerusalem, Antioch, and Rome) into abandoning his original idea that converts to Christianity should undergo circumcision.

9   *Padre Eterno*: Usually contracted to "Padreterno," literally "Eternal Father," God the Father.

9   *Michele Arcangiolo*: Michael the Archangel with an affectionate diminutive—Little Michael the Archangel.

9   *O Re dei secoli, immortale et invisibile*: O King of the Ages, immortal and invisible!

9   *Signor Iddio*: Lord God.

10   *O Re del Cielo*: O King of Heaven!

10   *La Sua Divina Maestà*: Your Divine Majesty (in Italian,

the third person is used instead of the second when addressing someone—here, God—in formal speech).

10 *O Dio Omnipotente*: O omnipotent God!

10 *lo Splendore Immortale della Sua Maestà*: The immortal splendor of Your Majesty.

11 *baldachino*: Canopy (usually spelled "baldacchino").

11 *Grand Turk*: The Sultan, the ruler of the Ottoman Empire.

12 *always being burnt down or blown up*: The 19th-century history of St. Paul-without-the-Walls is accurately predicted here. Although the church had maintained its original character for fourteen centuries, in 1823 while repairs were in progress on the roof, a fire gutted the building. It was restored in record time with help from such improbable sources as the Czar and the Pasha of Egypt. The Pasha or Viceroy of Egypt contributed pillars of alabaster, and perhaps this is the source of Toto's reference to the Grand Turk. The Pasha of Egypt in 1823 was the great general Muhammad Ali (1769-1849), founder of the city of Khartoum in the Sudan and patriarch of the dynasty only overthrown in 1953. Further damage was done to St. Paul-without-the-Walls in 1891 when an explosion in the nearby marketplace Porta Portese shattered the stained glass windows.

II. ABOUT THE LILIES OF SAN LUIGI

13 *San Sebastiano*: St. Sebastian, who was a member of the Praetorian Guard of the anti-Christian Emperor Diocletian (236-316), is the patron saint of athletes and soldiers and is a frequent subject of erotic art because of his martyrdom, pierced by arrows.

13 *San Pancrazio*: St. Pancratius or Pancras, the patron saint of children, is especially venerated in England because St. Augustine of Canterbury (d. 604) dedicated the first English church to him.

13   *Colosseo*: The famous Colosseum in Rome, where gladi-
     atorial battles were held and Christians were sacrificed.

14   *the prime of your life*: The saints in heaven traditionally
     have their ideal bodies restored to Edenic condition.

14   *always eighteen . . . always fourteen*: St. Sebastian was a
     soldier on active duty when he died, so he must have
     been relatively young although his exact age is un-
     recorded; St. Pancratius was martyred at fourteen. A
     similar saint is celebrated in Corvo's early poetry chap-
     book *Tarcissus: The Boy Martyr of Rome, in the Diocletian
     Persecution*.

14   *By Bacchus!*: A mild oath for a (pagan) Roman—Bacchus
     was the god of wine, the equivalent of the Greek
     Dionysus.

15   *San Luigi*: Not the famous St. Louis, the French crusader
     King Louis IX (1214-1270). In fact, the saint referred to
     here is known in English as St. Aloysius Gonzaga (1568-
     1591). The first of his given names was Luigi, but in
     keeping with the general European practice originating
     with the upper classes, he used the given name closest to
     his surname. Born into the royal family of Mantua (an
     independent duchy in northern Italy), he was a member
     of the Society of Jesus and is the patron saint of teen-
     agers (and more recently of AIDS patients). It was at
     the Church of St. Aloysius in Oxford that Corvo was
     received into the Roman Catholic Church in 1886. This
     Oxford church is associated with several other authors,
     including the early modernist poet Gerard Manley Hop-
     kins (1844-1889), who was parish priest there 1878-79, and
     the cultural historian Christopher Dawson (1889-1970),
     who was received into the Church there in 1914.

15   *the angel of San Sebastiano, who is called Sebastianello*:
     The guardian angel of St. Sebastian, who is called Sweet
     Little Sebastian. This is a curious nickname in light of
     the fact that seven pages further along Toto says that
     this angel is "as big as a giant."

15   *Jesuit*: Member of the Society of Jesus, a military order founded to aid in the Counter-Reformation and subsequently a politically troubling presence in many Roman Catholic countries.

15   *Iste Confessor*: "This Confessor," first words of a hymn originally composed in honor of St. Martin of Tours (c. 316-397), like St. Sebastian a Roman soldier who converted to Christianity, later a hermit and Bishop of Tours by acclamation.

16   *the Duomo*: Duomo means cathedral but is common shorthand for the Basilica di Santa Maria del Fiore, a famous architectural structure in Florence. The triptych on wood panels by Giovanni del Biondo in the Museo dell'Opera del Duomo is called "The Martyrdom of St. Sebastian and Scenes from His Life." The central panel shows the figure completely naked and pierced by arrows, but the archaic draftsmanship makes a less erotic impression than draped representations of St. Sebastian by Perugino, Sodoma, Rubens, Moreau, and others. Corvo himself wrote "Two Sonnets, for a Picture of Saint Sebastian the Martyr in the Capitoline Gallery, Rome." In this work, Corvo says of Sebastian, "Naked, but brave as a young lion can be, / Transfixed by arrows, he gains the victory." The painting he is describing is by Guido Reni (1575-1642).

18   *beautiful tunic of white wool with a broad purple stripe down the front*: The toga praetexta with a purple stripe was the distinctive garb of a Roman consul or senator.

18   *golden bulla*: An amulet worn around the neck of a boy in ancient Rome to ward off the evil eye.

18   *sandals of red leather*: Red sandals were the distinctive footwear of the Roman patrician class (the most elite of the nobles).

19   *festa*: Feast day, saint's day. The saint's day of St. Aloysius Gonzaga is 21 June, reasonably in season for lilies.

19   *one of the cherubini from the Aureola*: Cherubini are

cherubim—cherubs. The Aureola would presumably
be the real cloud of golden light that surrounds the
Godhead similar to the golden nimbus effect with this
name in the background behind many a painted repre-
sentation of a sacred person.

20 *Suprema Maestà e Grandezza*: Supreme Majesty and
Greatness.

20 *O Signor Iddio Altissimo*: O Highest Lord God!

21 *gita*: Outing, excursion.

21 *Genzano . . . Prince Francesco Sforza Cesarini had there
a palace with the most beautiful gardens in the world*: A
famous flower festival is still held in the town of
Genzano. The prince in question, among whose sub-
sidiary titles was Prince of Genzano, is undoubtedly
Francesco II Sforza Cesarini (1840-1899), Duke of
Segni, Senator of the Kingdom of Italy, and first Mayor
of Genzano in united Italy. Although his mother was
the Englishwoman Caroline Shirley, he descended in
many different lines from the old papal nobility.

22 *matins and lauds . . . meditation*: Matins and lauds are
daily prayers, respectively before dawn and at dawn,
but the terms are used in various looser ways. As a
Jesuit, St. Aloysius Gonzaga would practice structured
Ignatian meditation as described in *The Spiritual Exer-
cises* of St. Ignatius of Loyola (Íñigo Oñaz López de
Loyola, 1491-1556), the founder of the Society of Jesus.

22 *Sant'Agnese . . . San Vito and San Venanzio*: These are
all saints of the early Roman empire. St. Agnes was
a virgin martyred for dedicating her virginity to God.
St. Vitus is the patron saint of actors, comedians,
dancers, epileptics, and the Kingdom of Bohemia
(now the Czech Republic). He is the saint to pray to
in order to prevent oversleeping. Although there are
several saints named Venantius, the one meant here is
the patron Saint of Camerino, a principality in central
Italy north-northeast of Rome. The legend is that this

Saint Venantius was a seventeen-year-old martyred during the persecutions of the Emperor Decius (201-251). He was scourged and burned upside-down over a fire; then his teeth were knocked out, and his jaw was broken. Afterwards he was torn apart by lions and at last thrown from a high cliff.

22   *morra*: Morra is a guessing game that involves anticipating the number of fingers other players will throw out. Long associated with the town of Camerano (north-northeast of Rome but on the east coast of Italy), morra has a venerable history as a drinking game and such an intractable connection with gambling that it was banned for the last twenty years of the twentieth century.

23   *beads*: His rosary beads; he was praying.

24   *'Bastiano*: A nickname for Sebastian.

24   *Gardeners . . . have to stay up all the night between the twentieth and the twenty-first of June*: They are watching for thieves coming to steal flowers for the feast day of St. Aloysius Gonzaga.

24   *syringas*: The hydrangea bushes, so called after the nymph Syrinx, who escaped the god Pan by turning into the plant. He fashioned his musical pipes from the hollow reeds of the flower's stems.

27   *Church of San Luigi in Via Livia*: That is to say, the Church dedicated to St. Aloysius Gonzaga is on Livia Drusilla Street in Rome. Livia Drusilla (58 B.C.-A.D. 29) was the very controlling wife of the Emperor Augustus (63 B.C.-A.D. 14).

III. A CAPRICE OF THE CHERUBIM

28   *nine rows*: These are the traditional nine choirs of angels: from highest to lowest (although there is some disagreement about the order of precedence of the middle five categories) these are seraphim, cherubim,

thrones, dominations, virtues, powers, principalities, archangels, and ordinary or guardian angels.

28   *la Signora Duchessa*: If there is a reference to a specific Duchess here, it might be to Vittoria Colonna (1846-1939), wife of Francesco II Sforza Cesarini (1840-1899), Duke of Segni, but it is probably to his mother. In 1890 Corvo acquired an adoptive "grandmother" in the person of the dowager duchess Caroline. It is from her that he claimed to have received the title Baron. While it is sometimes assumed that he was lying or alternatively that she was joking, it is perhaps significant that her own status as a member of the Shirley family of the Earls Ferrers is enveloped in a similar difficulty. While she is often called "Lady Caroline Shirley" as appropriate to the daughter of an earl, and Robert Shirley, Earl Ferrers (1756-1827) left her a substantial legacy in his will, she was apparently born to the Earl's son and heir Robert Sewallis Shirley, Viscount Tamworth (1778-1824) out of wedlock. The legacy was the subject of a lawsuit in 1842 about the terms of the bequest, but the inquiry did not address the question of her identity. The dowager Duchess of Segni appears as the Countess of Santa Cotogna in the Epilogue to Corvo's book *Don Renato* and is praised there for her good deeds. And Corvo dedicated his sonnets on St. Sebastian to her.

29   *divel*: An obsolete form of "devil."

29   ✠: A symbol like this is common in missals (mass books) as an indication to make the sign of the cross.

29   *gardens of Palazzo Sforza Cesarini*: The famous gardens of this palace at Genzano are also mentioned in the story "About the Lilies of San Luigi."

30   *conquered the King of the divels*: The Archangel Michael, of course, led the forces of God against the rebellious fallen angels until (that is to say, only until) the intervention of the Christ brought an end to the conflict.

30   *the gate where hope must be laid down*: Dante describes
      the Gates of Hell as adorned with a lengthy warning
      ending "Lasciate ogne speranza, voi ch'intrate" (Aban-
      don All Hope, You Who Enter Here): *Inferno*, III. 9.

30   *Aeschmai Davi*: The name is untraced. The combina-
      tions "schm," "chm," and "hm" are all impossible in
      Italian, but the first word is somewhat like the Italian
      for Eskimo: "Eschimese." And the middle and end
      read as three words ("mai da vi") mean "never from
      you," an apt enough name for an imp.

30   *dæmon*: An obsolete form of "demon."

31   *Porta Pia*: The Porta Pia (City Gate of Pope Pius IV in
      the Aurelian Walls) is a monumental work of Michel-
      angelo's completed after his death.

31   *scimiotto*: A young ape.

31   *Gianetta*: Apparently a kitchen maid, perhaps a generic
      for such a person: Plain Joan.

32   *the lilac twigs you do use when I am disobedient*: This pas-
      sage suggests that the master practices the "English
      vice" on his servant—although gently.

32   *the Prince his garden*: Obsolete form of the possessive
      common in the Renaissance but based on a misap-
      prehension of possessives as contractions. Cf. Shake-
      speare's "Nor Mars his sword nor war's quick fire" in
      Sonnet 55.

33   *Leo*: The astrological sign, from the constellation Leo,
      the Lion. The sun is in Leo 23 July to 22 August, an
      appropriate time to take a dip in a fountain.

36   *chitarone*: Literally, "big guitar" from "chitarra," guitar.
      This is a specific instrument from the Baroque Period.
      Sometimes called the double guitar, it looks like two
      guitars of different sizes side by side. It has one sound
      box but two rose holes (of different sizes) and two
      necks.

36   *Donna Lina*: Probably a reference to the opera singer
      Lina Cavalieri (1874-1944). She was famous for the

smallness of her waist as a result of tight corseting, so the reference is not so much to swelling as in the other images as to the imminence of bursting out. Cavalieri did not make her opera debut until 1900, after *Toto* was published, but she was already a famous cabaret singer in her teens and went on to such predictable career accomplishments as being photographed for postcards, writing a book of beauty secrets, marrying a Russian prince, and appearing in silent movies.

36 *Ave*: The Ave Maria (Hail Mary) bell is a three-fold call to evening prayer. In *Religio Medici*, Sir Thomas Browne memorably writes that, although he is a Protestant, he "could never heare the *Ave Marie* Bell without an elevation."

38 *Benedicat vos omnipotens Deus* ✠ *Pater et* ✠ *Filius et* ✠ *Spiritus Sanctus*: May almighty God bless you—the Father and the Son and the Holy Ghost. This is the priest's (Latin) blessing of the congregation after mass.

IV. ABOUT BEATA BEATRICE AND THE MAMMA OF SAN PIETRO

39 *Macché!*: Of course not!

39 *Beatrice*: The name is perhaps chosen because it was the name of Dante's ethereal beloved.

39 *Toto jumped off the tree trunk*: This is the first internal use in the book of the name Toto. This is a proper saint's name as the Roman form of St. Theodore of Amasea (d. 306), a Greek soldier/martyr in the army of the Emperor Diocletian. St. Toto is the patron of Brindisi in southern Italy. Totò, with a closed terminal vowel, is also a diminutive for Salvatore in Sicily and for Antonio in the Campania. In the expanded collection *In His Own Image*, Toto has the surname Maidalchini. The chief historical association of the name Maidalchini is Olimpia Maidalchini Pamphili (1594-1657), notorious for looting the Vatican of treasures on

the death of her husband's brother Pope Innocent X
(1574-1655). The main model for the character Toto was
apparently named Toto Ephoros. Although Ephoros is
a Greek name, there was an historical Greek presence
in southern Italy. Some photographs of Toto Ephoros
by Corvo survive.

40   *Do you think that I spend what you give me at the wine shop
      or the tombola?*: The implication is that the master gives
      Toto money enough to save, not merely a reasonable
      wage. Tips for special services? Tombola is the game
      of bingo, but the reference is probably more generally
      to a betting parlor, properly an "allibratore."

40   *fritto . . . rigaglie*: "Fritto" just means fried. "Rigaglie"
      is chicken giblets without an indication of how they
      are cooked. So the whole culinary discussion may be
      about fried chicken livers.

42   *a couple of boys* [and the paean to androgyny that fol-
      lows]: Androgyny is the central image of Corvo's later
      book *The Desire and Pursuit of the Whole*.

43   *discolo*: Rascal.

43   *Abruzzi*: Although north of Rome on the east coast of
      Italy, the region of Abruzzi was part of the Kingdom
      of Two Sicilies and thus often regarded as a land of
      primitive people by inhabitants of the Papal States and
      places further north.

43   *Cellini's Perseus*: Benvenuto Cellini (1500-1571) is perhaps
      the greatest goldsmith of the Renaissance—or of all
      time. This is certainly his own opinion, as conveyed in
      his *Autobiography*. His larger-than-life statue "Perseus
      with the Head of Medusa" is, however, in bronze. It
      stands in the Loggia di Lanzi in Florence. Perseus is
      portrayed as a remarkably muscular ephebe (twenty-
      something lad) holding aloft the severed head of
      Medusa, the Gorgon with snakes in place of hair.

43   *Alban hills*: The Alban Hills (Colli Albani in Italian)
      are a range of dormant volcanos on the west coast

of southern Italy quite near Rome. They are called "Albani" (from the Latin for white) because the volcanic ash gives them a pale grayness.

43   *photographic and insect-hunting apparatus*: Biographical details that indicate the master narrating the Toto stories shares other tastes with Corvo than his appreciation of the ephebe. *In His Own Image* includes a version of this story with the additional detail identifying the master as "Don Friderico." That work also suggests that Toto did marry Beatrice and that she died in childbirth, bearing twins—details that ruin the beautiful ambiguity of this version.

44   *plump roundness of the Florentine Apollino*: The "Apollino" is another sculpture of an ephebe much celebrated in the nineteenth century. It was originally thought to be a Roman copy of something from the great ancient sculptor of such works, Praxiteles (fourth century B.C.). But a debate arose about whether a work presenting such a soft image of a young man could derive even at several removes from the cult of masculinity celebrated by the Praxitelean school.

45   *ennuyant*: Likely to induce boredom ("ennui" in French).

46   *Madonna del Portone*: Literally "Madonna at the Entrance," that is, the Assumption of the Blessed Virgin Mary into Heaven. A famous painting on this subject is "The Assumption of the Virgin" by Titian (1485-1576) in the Basilica of Santa Maria Gloriosa dei Frari in Venice. It is the largest altarpiece in that city.

46   *bastonatura*: Good thrashing.

46   *primrose*: The primrose is symbolic of first love. But, as a result, it often figures in warnings about the danger of losing control, as in Ophelia's mocking reply to the farewell warning of her brother Laertes. She hopes he is not like those who give sage advice but themselves tread "the primrose path to dalliance."

47   *donnicciuola*: Miserable little excuse for a woman.

47   *bellacuccia*: Pretty little one.

47   *Madonnina*: Little Madonna.

47   *mamma . . . to San Pietro*: There is no biblical informa-
     tion about the mother of St. Peter, but he is given a
     wife and mother-in-law (Matthew 8:14-17; Mark 1:29-
     31; Luke 4:38), and the immemorial slanders against
     mothers-in-law may be behind the story that follows.
     The story itself is a traditional folktale first recorded
     in a fifteenth-century German poem. Widely known
     throughout Europe, the story was included in a Sicilian
     version in Giuseppi Pitrè's 1875 collection *Fiabe, novelle,
     e racconti popolari siciliani*. This version is retold in Italo
     Calvino's *Fiabe italiane* (1956; translated by George
     Martin as *Italian Folktales*, 1980). This Sicilian version
     of the story is shorter than Corvo's, and the leek (as
     the vegetable is) is not bitten through by the mother
     of St. Peter but breaks in the struggle as she kicks back
     the other damned souls trying to escape from Hell.

47   *Santissimo Salvatore*: Most Holy Saviour.

47   *He went down to the seaside . . . to catch people's souls*:
     Matthew 4:18, Mark 1:16, Luke 5:1-2.

48   *Via Appia*: The Appian Way, the major road running
     from Rome down to Southern Italy since early impe-
     rial times, is named for its builder Appius Claudius
     Caecus (340 B.C.-273 B.C.) and is famous for paying no
     attention to the existing terrain and cutting a path
     straight through everything. Parts are still in use by
     automobile traffic.

49   *baiocco*: An obsolete coin, worth in Corvo's time about
     a halfpenny.

49   *Circus of Nero*: As a building a "Circus" is what we call
     a stadium. But it was a place of amusement for the
     ancients, although less innocent than a modern circus.
     Nero (37-68), one of the notoriously mad Roman
     Emperors of the early period, perfected the use of

public spectacles of cruelty to keep the people from objecting too much to his more bizarre behavior. Although smaller than the older Circus Maximus, it was the place of the early Christian martyrdoms, and for this reason St. Peter's Basilica now stands on the spot.

49   *cope . . . tiara . . . keys*: Three symbols of St. Peter's authority. As a bishop he dons a cope or episcopal cloak. As the first Pope, he wears the distinctive three-tiered crown or tiara that much later came to symbolize the secular authority of the Papacy. And as the guardian of the Gates of Heaven he holds the keys to the Kingdom.

50   *per l'Amore di Dio*: For the love of God. The apostrophe is on the wrong side of the "l" in the first edition. The phrase is in English in *The Yellow Book* version of this story.

51   *pasta in a copper pot*: The modern reader should not need to be told what pasta is or that it is the staple of Italian cuisine, but the reason for cooking in copper pots may have fallen out of awareness. Iron is bad for the taste of tomatoes and wine, two other staples of Italian cuisine. Traditionally, the best pots have had a thick layer of copper to heat quickly overlaid with a thin layer of tin so the copper can not react with acidic ingredients. Such copper pots are excellent for cooking quickly at high temperatures, as is appropriate with pasta.

V. ABOUT THE HERESY OF FRA SERAFICO

53   *'Cola*: A nickname for Nicola.

54   *camerata*: "Camerata" means both dormitory and comrade, and it perhaps means both here; that is to say, he went out with his schoolfellows.

54   *sixth commandment*: Following the numbering of St.

Augustine of Hippo (354-430), the Roman Catholic Church identifies the Commandment prohibiting adultery as the Sixth. The Anglican Church calls this Commandment the Seventh. By whatever number, it is understood to stigmatize lust and lustful thoughts with a synecdoche (part for the whole), and it is thus that Nicola supposes himself to become the near occasion of sin by allowing his stockings to fall down in public.

54 *Emissario*: Sewage drain pipe.

54 *holding a rhubarb leaf over his head*: As a sun screen.

55 *sub-deacon*: The lowest of the three degrees of holy orders in Roman Catholicism. Nicola is actually a cleric and has taken minor orders.

55 *And Geltruda, too!*: Perhaps a sister. Despite its Germanic look, this name is of Italian origin.

55 *Seminario*: Seminary, school to train young men for the priesthood.

55 *La Signora Duchessa*: This may be just a generalized reference to any great lady. If it has a specific reference to someone in Toto's world, it probably means the Duchess of Segni alluded to in the same way in story III, "A Caprice of the Cherubim."

55 *chierichetti*: Altar boys, acolytes.

56 *decano*: Deacon, the middle of the three degrees of holy orders, between sub-deacon and priest.

56 *abatino*: "Little abbot." An abbot is the head of a community of monks, so the nickname would be a joke indicating that Nicola is assuming a show of authority he does not deserve.

56 *Fra Serafico*: "Fra" means brother in the sense member of a religious order but not a priest. "Serafico" means seraphic (angelic) and is probably a made-up name appropriate to his eloquent preaching. A Fr. Serafico is a character in Corvo's early story "An Unforgettable Experience" (1894).

56   *of the Princes of Monte Corvino*: There is a famous Fran-
      ciscan named Giovanni di Monte Corvino (1246-1328).
      His eloquence converted many in China to Christian-
      ity. He is sometimes even credited with converting the
      Great Khan or Emperor of China and was certainly
      appointed and recognized as Archbishop of Peking
      (Beijing). This Franciscan seems not to have been from
      a princely family, and the reference here may simply be
      an indication of Corvo's own noble aspirations.

57   *son of San Francesco*: That is, a member of the Fran-
      ciscan Brotherhood, founded by St. Francis of Assisi
      (Giovanni di Bernardone 1181-1236). St. Francis is the
      patron saint of animals.

57   *fraticelli of his convent*: Little brothers of his religious
      order. St. Francis himself uses the term "fraticelli."
      "Convent" is more usual for a religious community of
      women, but it is not used so exclusively.

57   *prefer a shaved head and naked feet and to be a beggar*: The
      tonsure—full or at least partial shaving of the head—
      is a sign of humility that accompanies the taking of
      religious vows. Franciscans are famous for the rigor
      of their vow of poverty. One of the mock scholarly
      notes in the Corvo collaborative novel *The Weird of the
      Wanderer* is to the phrase "five-pointed tonsure": "The
      tonsure is, of course, not pentagonal but circular. The
      bishop who confers it does, however, ceremonially dip
      the clerk's hair in five places, *e.g.* front, back, right, left,
      and crown, while teaching the tonsured to twitter:
      'Dominus pars—haereditatis meae—et calicis meis—
      Tu es Qui restitues—haereditem meam mihi [Psalms
      15:5 in the Vulgate—16:5 in Protestant Bibles—literally,
      Lord, Portion of my inheritance and of my goblet,
      Thou it is Who wilt restore my inheritance to me].'
      Hence, perhaps, the epithet 'five-pointed.'—A.H. [the
      supposed editor Adam Howley]."

57   *Dumbtongue*: Probably an allusion to an early nickname

of St. Thomas Aquinas (1225-1274), the great theologian. Aquinas, author of the famous *Summa Theologica* ("The Most Important Theological Ideas") was called The Dumb Ox before his eloquence was understood. Toto seems to be stringing together bits of information about many famous religious figures.

57 *the Fra Guardiano*: The definite article indicates that this is the brother's office and not his name. He is the Warder or Housemaster who keeps track of everyone's comings and goings and makes sure that the students are in their rooms when they are supposed to be.

58 *fervorini*: Endearing bursts of fervor and enthusiasm.

58 *Papa Silvio*: "Papa" means Pope, and "Silvio" is Silvanus in Latin and Selwyn or Silas in English. There was a Pope Silvanus (536-537), but the allusion is probably to Pius II (1405-1464), whose birth name was Enea Silvio di Piccolomini. Since he was already a popular erotic novelist at the time of his election (1458), he was often referred to affectionately by his real given name (that is, the one closest to his surname). His literary works include *Euryalus and Lucretia; or, The Story of Two Lovers* and an autobiography published while he was Pope, *Commentaries*.

58 *preach the Lent*: Preach the keynote sermon on self-denial at the beginning of Lent, the forty days of penitence that lead up to Easter.

58 *Church of San Carlo al Corso*: San Carlo is St. Charles (often Carlo even in English) Borromeo (1538-1584), nephew of Pope Pius IV, Cardinal, Archbishop of Milan. He is the patron saint of seminarians, apple orchards, and the Kingdom of Lombardy (Duchy of Milan). The Church of San Carlo al Corso, one of the major historic basilicas of Rome, is quite near the famous Trevi Fountain and the equally famous Spanish Steps of the Franciscan Church of Trinità dei Monti. Corso is the street so named because it was a race course during

the Renaissance. In the nineteenth century this was the English Quarter of Rome. John Keats and Percy Bysshe Shelley and Henry James all lived here. When the book was written, the area was the center of the fashionable shopping district of the city. In 1889, the Franciscan Padre Agostino da Montefeltro (1839-1921) preached a celebrated series of Lenten sermons at San Carlo al Corso.

59 *Tonto Pappagallo*: A made-up name. It means Dumbbell the Parrot.

59 *apsis*: Apse, a semi-circular, domed projection of a church or other building.

61 *Seraficone mio*: Great Serafico. Since Toto has described Serafico as physically "little," the augmentative "-one" is an insult. The "mio," meaning "my" but coming after the name, is a kind of mocking endearment: "My dear Serafico." If genuinely honorific, "Mio" would come before the noun and (since this is not a member of the family) be accompanied by the definite article: "Il mio padre Serafico."

61 *Campo di Fiore*: Literally, "Field of Flowers." It is a specific location in Rome, a big marketplace. The sense is "in public."

61 *Sant'Uffizio*: The Holy Office, the judicial arm of the Papacy, in full the Sacred Congregation of the Holy Office, now called the Congregation for the Doctrine of the Faith and historically the Roman Inquisition.

61 *the Grand Inquisitor*: The head of the Holy Office, now called the Prefect.

62 *eminence*: Correct title of address to a cardinal (electoral prince of the Church).

62 *Princes Colonna and Orsini*: The princely families of Colonna and Orsini are among the oldest of the papal nobility, and their hostility to one another is a staple of the history of the medieval Church. It was, in fact, by bringing about a reconciliation between the two fami-

lies that Enea Silvio di Piccolomini earned election to the papacy as Pius II in 1458.

62 *scarlet cardinals*: Scarlet is the distinctive color of the ecclesiastical vestments of cardinals.

62 *bishops by the score in purple and green*: Purple is the distinctive color of the ecclesiastical vestments of bishops. Green is the color of the stole and chasuble used by clergy saying mass during "ordinary" time (that is, not on feast days of a particular character). The symbolic hat atop the coat of arms of a national patriarch is green.

62 *friars grey, friars white, friars black*: Gray friars are Franciscans; white friars are Carmelites (observing the rule of St. Albert Avogadro (1149-1214), Latin Patriarch of Jerusalem); black friars are Dominicans (observing the rule of St. Dominic Guzman y Aza, c. 1170-1221).

64 *Beato Padre Francesco*: Beatified Father Francis of Assisi. Beatification is a step in the process of achieving sainthood. St. Francis was canonized as a saint in 1228, only two years after his death, so Fra Serafico is using the term "Beato" somewhat loosely.

65 *O Clementissimo Signor Iddio*: O most lenient Lord.

65 *San Gregorio*: St. Gregory I the Great (c. 540-604), Pope, author of *On Pastoral Care*.

65 *Celeste Iddio*: Heavenly Lord.

65 *Homily*: Formal spiritual advice addressed by a preacher to a congregation, especially when the topic is interpretation of a biblical text, as it is here.

65 *San Luca*: St. Luke the Evangelist.

66 *Doctors of the Church*: Doctor of the Church is a specific category of sainthood and accurately applied here to St. Gregory the Great. Others mentioned in this book with the title are St. Augustine of Hippo and St. Thomas Aquinas. The image of the Doctors of the Church sitting is a row is taken from Dante's *Paradiso*.

67 *O Dio, Padre delle misericordie*: O God, Father of All Mercies.

67   *seven archangels*: There is some question about the total number of archangels. While angels as such are infinite in number—or at least uncountable through human intelligence—only seven archangels are known to mankind by name: Michael, Gabriel, Raphael, Uriel, Selaphiel, Jegudiel, and Barachiel. Since the specific function of an archangel is to be an intermediary between God and man, are the archangels who are known the sum of those who exist? Of the seven traditional names, only Michael has an undisputed claim to the rank. Seven is a traditional sacred number.

67   *Apostolic College*: Apostolic College conventionally means the original twelve apostles as the first Ecumenical Council, the first gathering of leaders of the Church inspired by God to make rules for the Church free from the possibility of error. But St. Paul was not part of this original group, and it is hard to imagine what business such a group would have to conduct in Heaven. Toto may be imagining the saints in Heaven as gathering with their earthly cronies to talk over old times.

67   *the man who made them Christians in England, sir, and the chant*: St. Augustine of Canterbury is the Apostle of the English, but St. Gregory the Great is credited with sending him on this mission after having seen captive Angle boys and punningly commented on their resemblance to angels. The story is told by the Venerable (now St.) Bede (673-735) in his *Ecclesiastical History of the English People*. St. Gregory the Great is also responsible for the unaccompanied church choral music called Gregorian Chant.

68   *Mola*: A bridge built by the Emperor Hadrian (76-138, one of the Five Good Emperors). It was while crossing Il Ponte della Mola that St. Gregory the Great saw a vision of Michael the Archangel rescuing a soul from the devil.

68   *O Principio de ogni cosa*: O First Cause of All Things!

68   *second letter to San Timoteo*: Paul's Second Epistle to Tim-
      othy: 2 Timothy 2:5. The 1582 Douay-Rheims Roman
      Catholic New Testament translates the verse as "For
      he also that striveth for the mastery, is not crowned,
      except he strive lawfully." The "strive" (which is also in
      the King James translation) considerably weakens the
      case for reading the passage as advocating martyrdom
      although the verses just before do refer to serving as a
      soldier for Christ.

69   *the Apostle of the Gentiles and the Apostle of England*:
      St. Paul is the Apostle to the Gentiles for focusing his
      work on reaching beyond the Jewish community for
      converts. St. Augustine of Canterbury is the Apostle
      to the English, although under the direction of St.
      Gregory, as already indicated. Corvo painted a banner
      depicting this St. Augustine; it hangs in St. Winefride's
      Well museum in Holywell, Wales.

69   *Canonical Books*: Books accepted as inspired by the
      Holy Ghost and finding a place in the Bible. The
      canon of books in the Roman Catholic Bible includes
      not only the Hebrew Bible and the New Testament
      accepted by all Christians but also a Deuterocanon
      of late Jewish works written in Greek. These works
      are called the Apocrypha (Doubtful Works) by Protes-
      tants. Many other religious works survive from early
      Christianity (New Testament Apocrypha). There was
      little public awareness of the existence of these other
      non-canonical works until recently, but of late they
      have become the subject of much interest in popular
      culture.

69   *Maestà Coeterna dell'Adorabile Trinità*: Co-Eternal
      Majesty of the Trinity All Adore.

70   *O Potenza Infinita*: O Infinite Power!

71   *Evviva, evviva, Bocca d'Oro, evviva, evviva*: Hurrah,
      hurrah, Golden Mouth, hurrah, hurrah!

VI. ABOUT ONE WAY IN WHICH CHRISTIANS LOVE
ONE ANOTHER

72   *Fra Leone of the Cappuccini*: Capuchins are members of
     the Order of Friars Minor, so called from their distinc-
     tive hoods (caps). The order was founded in 1520 when
     Matteo da Bascio of the Franciscans sought a return to
     a fuller practice of poverty as originally proposed by
     St. Francis. The name Fra Leone may be a nod to the
     fact that Capuchins have a long history of work in the
     west African colony (now country) Sierra Leone.

72   *impertinence of bronze*: The sense is that the Capuchins
     are third rate, not gold or silver but claiming to be.

72   *Simon Something-or-other*: Toto is probably thinking of
     Simon Magus, the first Christian heretic. He is men-
     tioned in Acts 8:14-25.

72   *round tippet, etc.*: An ecclesiastical vestment like the
     stole. The stole is worn while saying mass, the tippet
     while preaching. But the terminological distinction
     is characteristic of Anglican worship, not Roman
     Catholic. Since Friars are not priests, the stoles they
     do wear might plausibly be called tippets. The sartorial
     distinctions are a consequence of the separation of the
     Capuchins from the Franciscans, not their cause. The
     roundness of the Franciscan stole is the shape of the
     part behind the neck. To judge from Chaucer's pilgrim
     Friar, Franciscans were not above storing things in the
     stole: "His tippet was ay farsed full of knives / And
     pinnes, for to yiven faire wives," *The Canterbury Tales*,
     "General Prologue," 233-234.

74   *five Paters, and five Aves, and five Glorias*: These are
     prayers (phrased as a typical penance given in confes-
     sion) identified by the first word in the Latin version
     of each: "Pater Noster" ("Our Father"—"The Lord's
     Prayer"), Ave Maria ("Hail Mary"), and "Gloria in

Excelsis Deo" ("Glory to God in the Highest"—"The Gloria").

75   *enjoy myself in the orchard*: By stealing fruit. Perhaps having been caught doing this in the past accounts for Toto's antagonism to the Capuchins. The episode, including the explanation for the nudity, is based on a real incident involving an Amadeo Amadei and described in one of *The Venice Letters* of Corvo's to Charles Masson Fox (1866-1935).

76   *nothing but stick*: Nothing but being caned—beaten with a stick.

76   *De Profundis*: "From the Depths," the first words of the Latin version of Psalm 129 (in the traditional Roman Catholic numbering based on the Greek text; this is number 130 in the Hebrew Bible). "De Profundis" is one of seven Penitential Psalms: "De profundis clamavi ad te Domine" ("From the depths, I cried to you, Lord!").

80   *baptized the baby herself*: A perfectly canonical practice. The "usual minister" of baptism is a priest, but the sacrament is valid if it includes the intention to baptize, if the water is flowing, and if the sign of the cross is used. Naming is not a necessary element. A major scandal arose on this subject in the middle of the nineteenth century and became a catalyst in the unification of Italy. In 1858, the six-year-old Jewish boy Edgardo Mortara was seized by the Papal authorities and taken from his parents after it became known that he had been baptized by a servant girl when on the point of death as an infant. Pope Pius IX (1792-1878) had the child raised as a Catholic, and the case became an international scandal, diminishing Italian and European support for maintaining the political independence of the Papal States.

[COLOPHON]

84   *of the nine and forty*: In His Own Image includes twenty-

four additional Toto stories, but it is doubtful that Corvo wrote the full number given here.

84   *John Lane*: The first publisher of these stories in journal form and as a book. Lane is also responsible for the title of the collection, which Corvo originally wanted to call *A Sensational Atomist*. For what Corvo perceived as a certain meanness in the terms he negotiated with authors, Lane (1854-1925) is pilloried as Slim Schelm in *Nicholas Crabbe*, being described as "a tubby little potbellied bantam, scrupulously attired and looking as though he had been suckled on bad beer." While Lane did see publishing primarily as a way of making money, he was responsible for bringing out many controversial works, including the journal *The Yellow Book*, in which the Toto stories in this book were first printed as follows:

"About Beata Beatrice and the Mamma of San Pietro." 9 (1896): 93-101.
"About One Way in Which Christians Love One Another." 11 (1896): 155-162.
"About San Pietro and San Paolo." 7 (1895): 209-214.
"About the Heresy of Fra Serafico." 11 (1896): 143-155.
"About the Lilies of San Luigi." 7 (1895): 214-224.
"A Caprice of the Cherubim." 9 (1896): 86-92.

84   *Corvicastra in Aria*: Corvo Castle in the Air.

84   *Saint Dismas*: The name given to one of the thieves crucified with the Christ because he repented his sins and asked Jesus to remember him in the Kingdom of the next world (Matthew 27:38).

84   *m viijc xc viij*: Roman numerals quirkily reinterpreted. The first and third terms are straightforward Roman numerals, the first for 1000 and the third for 90 (c for 100 with x for 10 in front to be subtracted). The fourth term is 8 (v for 5 with i for 1 added afterwards three

times); the j represents a traditional scribal convention for making a decorative flourish with a terminal i. These three sets of symbols could have been run together for a total of 1098 (mxcviii). The second set of apparent Roman numerals here presents a problem. It must represent 800 to give the grand total 1898, the year the book was published. But to do so, we would need to multiply viij by c despite the fact that the ancient Romans (and the neo-Latin writers after them) did not have a way of doing multiplication as a calculation with these symbols (although a line over a symbol does multiply it by a thousand). In addition, v is not allowed in subtractions, j is not used in the middle of a number, and the spaces are not meaningful without a knowledge of the place-holding convention of Arabic numbers. The proper Roman numeral for 1898 is mdcccxcviii: 1 thousand plus 500 plus 100 three more times plus another 100 with 10 subtracted from before it and then 5 added followed by 1 three times.

84   *lx i*: The Roman numeral for 61 (50 plus 10 plus 1) with a Corvine space but without the scribal flourish. The space is between the l and the xi in the first edition, but this usage contradicts the system Corvo has just established, requiring a space between the lx and the i to represent the decimal places of Arabic numbers. The English sense, of course, requires, not a cardinal number, but the ordinal number "sixty-first."

84   *Queen Victoria*: Victoria (1819-1901), Queen of the United Kingdom of Great Britain and Ireland and Empress of India. Her long reign came to an end shortly after the publication of *Stories Toto Told Me*.